'It's OK, I'm wearing really big knickers!'

Fabulously funny!

Further Confessions of Georgia Nicolson:

Angus, thongs and full-frontal snogging

'It's OK, I'm wearing really big knickers!'

'Knocked out by my nunga-nungas.'

'Dancing in my nuddy-pants!'

'...and that's when it fell off in my hand.'

'...then he ate my boy entrancers.'

Also available on tape and CD:

'...and that's when it fell off in my hand.'

'...then he ate my boy entrancers.'

'It's OK, I'm wearing really big knickers!'

Fabulously funny!

Louise Rennison

HarperCollins *Children's Books*

Find out more about Georgia at
www.georgianicolson.com

This edition produced for The Book People Ltd,
Hall Wood Avenue, Haydock, St Helens WA11 9UL

First published in Great Britain by Piccadilly Press Ltd, 2000
Published by Scholastic Ltd, 2001
This edition published by HarperCollins *Children's Books*, 2005
HarperCollins *Children's Books* is a division of HarperCollins*Publishers* Ltd,
77-85 Fulham Palace Road, Hammersmith, London W6 8JB

The HarperCollins *Children's Books* website address is
www.harpercollinschildrensbooks.co.uk

ISBN-13 978-0-00-776963-6
ISBN-10 0-00-776963-6

Printed and bound in England by
Clays Ltd, St Ives plc

To my dear family: Mutti, Vati, Sophie, Libbs, Hons, Eduardo Delfonso Delgardo, John S, Apee, Francesbirginia and especially Kimbo. Thanks you all for not killing me yet.

Also dedicated to my mates: Salty Dog, Jools, Jedbox, Badger, Elton, Jimjams, Jenks, Phil, Bobbins, Lozzer, the Mogul, Fanny, Dear GeH. MSH, Porky, Morgan, Alan D, Liz G, Tony G, Psychic Sue, Roge the Doge and Barbara D and the Ace Crew from school, Kim and Cock of the North xxxxxx.

An especial thank you to John, the Pope. Where would I have been without your wise advice – "Stop making such a fuss and just get on with it, you silly girl!"?

Heartfelt thanks and sympathy to Brenda, Jude, Emma and all the very fab people at Piccadilly.

And of course to Gillon and Clare – HURRAH!!

The Sex God has landed... and, er, taken off again

Sunday July 18th
My room
6:00 p.m.

Staring out of my bedroom window at other people having a nice life.

Who would have thought things could be so unbelievably pooey? I'm only fourteen and my life is over because of the selfishosity of so-called grown-ups. I said to Mum, "You are ruining my life. Just because yours is practically over there is no reason to take it out on me."

But as usual when I say something sensible and meaningful she just tutted and adjusted her bra like a Russian roulette player. (Or do I mean disco thrower? I don't know and, what's more, I don't care.) If I counted up the number of times I've been tutted at... I could open a tutting shop. It's just SO not fair... How can my parents take me away from my mates and make me go to New Zealand? Who goes to New Zealand?

In the end, when I pointed out how utterly useless as a mum she was, she lost her rag and SHOUTED at me.

"Go to your room right now!"

I said, "All right, I'll go to my ROOM!! I WILL go to my room!! And do you know what I'll be doing in my room? No you don't, so I'll tell you! I'll be just BEING in my room. That's all. Because there is nothing else to do!!!!!!"

Then I just slammed off. Left her there. To think about what she has done.

Unfortunately it means that I am in my bed and it is only six o'clock.

7:00 p.m.
Oh Robbie, where are you now? Well, I know where you are now actually, but is this any time to go away on a footie trip?

On the bright side I am now the girlfriend of a Sex God.

7:15 p.m.
On the dark side, the Sex God doesn't know his new

girlfriend is going to be forced to go to the other (useless) side of the universe in a week's time.

7:18 p.m.
I can't believe that after all the time it has taken to trap the SG, all the make-up I have had to buy, the trailing about, popping up unexpectedly when he was out anywhere... all the planning... all the dreaming – it's gone to waste. I finally get him to snog me (number six) and he says, "Let's see each other but keep it quiet for a bit." And at that moment, with classic poo timing, Mutti says, "We're off to New Zealand next week."

My eyes are all swollen up like mice eyes from crying. Even my nose is swollen. It's not small at the best of times, but now it looks like I've got three cheeks. Marvellous. Thank you, God.

9:00 p.m.
I'll never get over this.

9:10 p.m.
Time goes very slowly when you are suicidal.

9:15 p.m.

I put sunglasses on to hide my tiny mincers. They are new ones that Mum bought me in a pathetic attempt to interest me in going to Kiwi-a-gogo land. They looked quite cool, actually. I looked a bit like one of those French actresses who smoke Gauloise and cry a lot in between snogging Gerard Depardieu. I tried a husky French accent in the mirror.

"And zen when I was, how you say? *Une teen-ager, mes parents, mes très, très horriblement parents*, take me to *Nouvelle Zelande*. Ahh *merde!*"

At which point I heard Mum coming up the stairs and had to leap into bed. She popped her head round the door and said, "Georgie... are you asleep?"

I didn't say anything. That would teach her.

As she left she said, "I wouldn't sleep in the sunglasses if I were you, they might get embedded in your head."

What kind of parenting was that? Mum's medical knowledge was about as good as Dad's DIY. And we had all seen his idea of a shed. Before it fell down on Uncle Eddie.

Eventually I was drifting off into a tragic snooze when I heard shouting coming from next door's garden. Mr and Mrs Next Door were out there, banging and shouting and

10

throwing things about. Is this really the time for noisy gardening? They have no consideration for those who might want to sleep because they have tragedy in their life. I felt like opening the window and shouting, "Garden more quietly, you loons!"

But then I couldn't be bothered getting out of my snuggly bed of pain.

Police raid
Mucho excitemondo
12:10 a.m.

When the doorbell rang I shot out of bed and looked down the stairs. Mum had opened the door wearing a nightdress that you could quite easily see through! Even if you didn't want to. Which I didn't. She has no pride. There were a couple of policemen standing at the door. The bigger one was holding a sack up in front of him at arm's length and his trousers were shredded round the ankles.

"Is this your bloody cat?" he enquired, not very politely for a public servant.

Mum said, "Well, I... er."

I ran down the stairs and went to the door.

"Good evening, constable. This cat, is it about the size of a small Labrador?"

He said, "Yes."

I nodded encouragingly and went on. "And has it got tabby fur and a bit of its ear missing?"

PC Plod said, "Er... yes."

And I said, "No, it's not him then, sorry."

Which I thought was very funny indeed. The policeman didn't.

"This is a serious business, young lady."

Mum was doing her tutting thing again, and combining it with head shaking and basooma adjusting. Deeply unattractive. I thought the policeman might be distracted by her and say, "Go and put some clothes on, madam," but he didn't, he just kept going on at me.

"This thing has had your neighbours penned up in their greenhouse for an hour. They managed to dash into the house eventually but then it rounded up their poodles."

"Yes, he does that. He is half Scottish wildcat. He hears the call of the wilds sometimes and then he..."

"You should keep better control of it."

He went moaning on in a policemany way for hours

and hours. I said, as patiently as I could, although I had enough things to think about as it was, "Look, I'm being made to go to Whangamata by my parents. It is at the other, more useless, side of the universe. It is in New Zealand. Have you seen *Neighbours*? Is there nothing you can do for me?"

My mum gave me her worst look and said, "Don't start, Georgia, I'm not in the mood."

The policeman didn't seem "in the mood" either. He said, "This is a serious warning. You keep this thing under control otherwise we will be forced to take sterner measures."

Mum was hopeless as per usual. She started smiling and fiddling with her hair.

"I'm really sorry to have troubled you, inspector. Would you like to come in and have a nightcap or something?"

It was so EMBARRASSING. He probably thought we ran a brothel in our spare time. The "inspector" was all smiling and he said, "That's very kind of you, madam, but we have to get on. Protecting the public from vicious criminals, dangerous moggies, and so on."

I didn't say anything as I took the wiggling sack, I just looked ironically at his chewed trousers.

Mum went BERSERK about Angus. She said, "He'll have to go."

I said, "Oh yes, perfect, just take everything that I love and destroy it. Just think of your own self and make me go halfway round the universe and lose the only boy I love. You can't just leave Sex Gods, you know, they have to be kept under constant surveillance and..."

She had gone into her bedroom.

Angus strolled out of the bag and strutted around the kitchen looking for a snack. He was purring like two tanks. Libby wandered in all sleepy with her blankin'. Her night-time nappy was bulging round her knees. The last thing I needed was a poo explosion at this time of night so I said, "Go tell Mummy about your pooey nap-naps, Libby."

But she just said, "Shhh, bad boy," and went over to Angus. She kissed him on the nose and then sucked it before she dragged him off to bed.

I don't know why he lets her do anything she likes with him. He almost had my hand off the other day when I tried to take his plate away and he hadn't quite finished.

Monday July 19th

11:00 a.m.

I am feeling sheer desperadoes. It's a day and a half now since I snogged the Sex God. I think I have snog withdrawal. My lips keep puckering up.

I HAVE to find a way of not going to Kiwi-a-gogo land. I went on hunger-strike this morning. Well, apart from a Jammy Dodger.

2:00 p.m.

Phone rang.

Mum yelled up at me, "Gee, will you get that, love? I'm in the bath."

I yelled back, "You can wash the outside clean, but you can't wash the inside!"

She yelled again, "Georgia!!!"

Dragged myself up from my bed of pain and went all the way downstairs and picked up the phone.

"I said, "Hello, Heartbreak Hotel here," and all I could hear was just crackle, crackle, surf, swish, swish. So I shouted really loudly, "HELLO, HELLO, HELLO!!!!" and this faraway voice said, "Bloody hell!"

It was my father, or Vati as I call him. Phoning from New Zealand. He was, as usual, in a bad mood for no reason.

"Why did you shout down the phone? My ears are all ringing now."

I said, reasonably enough, "Because you didn't say anything."

"I did, I said hello."

"Well I didn't hear you."

"Well you can't have been listening properly."

"How can I not listen properly when I am answering the phone?"

"I don't know, but if anyone can manage it, you can."

Oh, play the old record again, it's always me that does things wrong. I said, "Mum's in the bath."

He said, "Just a minute, don't you want to know how I am?"

"Er, let me guess... funny moustache, bit bulky round the bottom department?"

"Don't be so bloody cheeky! Get your mum. I give up on you. I don't know what you learn at that school besides how to put on lipstick and be cheeky."

I put the phone down because he can grumble on like

that for centuries if you let him. I shouted, "Mutti, there is a man on the phone. He claims to be my dear vati but I don't think he is because he was quite surly with me."

Mum came out of the bathroom with her hair all wet and dripping and in just a bra and pants. She really has got the most gigantic basoomas, I'm surprised she doesn't topple over. Good Lord.

I said, "I am at a very impressionable age, you know."

She just gave me her worst look and grabbed the phone. As I went through the door I could hear her saying, "Hello, darling. What? I know. Oh I know. You needn't tell me that... I have her all the time. It's a nightmare."

That's nice talk, isn't it?

As I point out to anyone who will listen (i.e. no one), I didn't ask to be born. I am only here because she and Vati... urgh... anyway, I won't go down that road.

My room
2:10 p.m.
I could hear her rambling on to Dad, going, "Hmmm – well I know, Bob... I know... Uh huh... I KNOW... I know. Yes, I know..."

In the name of pantyhose, what are grown-ups like? I shouted down to her, "Break the news to him gently that I'm definitely not in a TRILLION years coming."

He must have heard me because even upstairs I could hear muffled shouting from down the other end of the phone. I wasn't amazed by the shouting as my vati is prone to violence. Once I poured aftershave into his lager and lime when he was out of the room. For a merry joke. But he didn't get the joke. When he stopped choking he went all ballisticisimus and shouted, "You complete IDIOT!!!" really loudly at me. It's the kind of thing that will cost me hundreds of pounds in therapy fees in later life. (Should I have a life, which I don't.)

2:30 p.m.

Playing sad songs in my bedroom, still in my jimjams.

Mutti came into my room and said, "Can I come in?"

I said, "No."

But that didn't put her off.

She came and sat on the edge of my bed and put her hand on my foot. I said, "Owww!!!"

She said, "Look, love, I know this is all a bit complicated, especially at your age, but this is a really big opportunity for us. Your dad thinks he has a real chance to make something of himself over in Whangamata."

I said, "what's wrong with the way he is now? Quite a few people like fat blokes with ridiculous moustaches. You do."

She came on all parenty then. "Georgia, don't think that rudeness is funny because it isn't."

"It can be."

"No it isn't."

"Well you laughed when Libby called Mr Next Door 'nice tosser'."

"Well Libby is only three and she thinks that tosser is like Bill or Dad or something. Can't you see this trip as an exciting adventure?"

"What, like when you are on your way to school and then suddenly you get run over by a bus and have to go to hospital, or something?"

"Yes, like when... NO!! Come on, Georgie, try to be a pal, just for me."

I didn't say anything.

"You know that your dad can't get a job here. What else is he supposed to do? He's only trying to look after us all."

After a bit she sighed and went out.

Life is *très merde* and double bum. Why doesn't Mutti understand I can't leave now? She can be ludicrously dim. It's not her that I get my intelligence from. It is certainly no thanks to her that I came top in... er... well anyway, it's nothing to do with her what I do. I am just the unfortunate recipient of some of her genes. The orang-utan eyebrow gene, for instance. She has to do a lot of plucking to keep her eyebrows apart and she has selfishly passed it on to me. Since I shaved mine off by mistake last term they seem to have gone even more haywire and akimbo. The shaving has encouraged them to grow about a metre a week. If I left them alone I'd be blind by October. Jas has got ordinary eyebrows, why can't I?

Also, while I am on the subject, the worst news of all is that I think I have inherited her breast genes. My basoomas are definitely growing. I am very worried that I may end up with huge breasts like hers. Everyone notices hers.

Once, when we were on the ferry to France, Dad said to Mum, "Don't stand too near to the edge, Connie, otherwise your chest might be declared a danger to shipping."

5:00 p.m.

I've just had a flash of whatsit!! It's so obvious, I am indeed a genius! Simple pimple. I'll just tell Mum that I'll stay behind and... LOOK AFTER THE HOUSE!! The house can't just be left empty for months because... er... squatters might come in and take it over. Anarchists who will paint everything black, including, probably, Mr and Mrs Next Door's poodles. They'll be begging for Angus to come back.

Excellent, brilliant fabulosa idea!! Mum will definitely see the sense of it.

I'll promise to be really mature and grown-up and responsible. I mainly want to stay in England because of the terrifically good education system. That is how I will sell it to Mutti.

"Mutti," I will say, "this is a crucial time in my schooldays. I think I may be picked for the hockey team."

Thank goodness I didn't bother Mum with my school report from last term. I saved her the trouble of reading it by signing it myself.

5:05 p.m.

You would think that Hawkeye could think of something more imaginative to write than, *Hopelessly childish attitude in class.* Just because she caught me doing my (excellent) impression of a lockjaw germ.

5:10 P.M.
I could have groovy parties that everyone would really want to come to. I'm going to make a list of all the people I will ask to the parties:

<u>First – Sex Gods</u>
Robbie... er, that's it.

<u>Second – the Ace Crew</u>
Rosie, Jools, Ellen and, I suppose, Jas if she pulls her pants up and makes a bit more effort with me. She has been a bit of a Slack Alice on the pal front since she got Tom.

<u>Third – close casuals</u>
Mabs, Sarah, Abbie, Phebes, Hattie, Bella... people I like for a laugh but wouldn't necessarily lend my mum's leather jacket to... then acquaintances and fanciable brothers.

5:20 p.m.

I may even allow crap dancers like Sven to come if they have pleasing or amusing personalities (and gifts).

5:23 p.m.

I tell you who I won't be asking – Nauseating P. Green, that's who. She is definitely banned. If I am made to sit next to her again next term I will definitely kill myself. Why is she so boring? She does it deliberately to annoy me. She breeds hamsters. What is the matter with her?

Who else will be on the exclusion list? Wet Lindsay, Robbie's ex. It would be cruel to invite her and let her see Robbie and me being so happy and snogging in front of her, etc. Also she would kill me and that would spoil the party atmosphere.

Who else? Oh, I know, Jackie and Alison, otherwise known as the Bummer Twins. They can't come because they are too common.

9:10 p.m.

Looking out of my window. I can see Mark, the boy with the biggest gob in the universe, going off to town with his mates. People are out there having fun. I hate that. I haven't got any real friends – as soon as a boy comes along they just forget about me, it's pathetic.

I could never be that shallow.

I wonder if the Sex God is having second thoughts about me because of my nose?

9:15 p.m.

Jas phoned. Tearing herself away from Tom for a second. She said, "Have you told her you are not going, yet?"

"No, I try but she takes no notice. I told her that it is a very important time for me as I am fourteen and poised on the brink of womanhood."

"On the what?"

Jas can be like half girl, half turnip. I said, "Do you remember what our revered headmistress, Slim, said at the end of summer term? She said, 'Girls, you are poised on the brink of womanhood, which is why I want to see no more false freckles painted on noses. It is silly and it isn't funny or dignified.'"

"False freckles are funny."

"I know."

"Well why would Slim say they weren't?"

"Jas."

"What?"

"Shut up now."

9:30 p.m.

I've got Libby, her scuba-diving Barbie doll, which has arms like steel forks, and her Thomas the Tank Engine, all in my bed. It's like sleeping in a toy box only not so comfortable. Plus Libby has been making me play Eskimo kissing; it has made my nose really sore. I said, "Libby, that's enough Eskimo now," but she just said, "Kwigglkwoggleugug," which I suppose she thinks is Eskimo.

What is the matter with my life? Why is it so deeply unfab?

10:00 p.m.

Looking at the sky outside my window and all the stars. I thought of all the people in history and so on who have been sad and have asked God for help. I fell to my knees (which was a bit painful as I landed on a plate of jam sandwiches I had left by my bed). Through my tears I prayed, "Please, God, let the phone ring and let it be Robbie. I promise I will go to church all the time if he rings. Thank you."

Midnight

So much for Our Vati in Heaven. What on earth is the point of asking God for something if you don't get it?

Decided to buy a Buddha tomorrow.

1:00 a.m.

As time is short it might be all right to ask Buddha for something before I actually invest in a statue of him.

I don't really know how to speak to Buddha. I hope he understands English. I expect, like most deities, it's more a sort of reading your thoughts job.

1:30 a.m.

Because I haven't been a practising Buddhist for long (half an hour) I'll restrict my requests to the essentials.

Which are:

1. When I suggest to Mum that she leaves me behind to look after the house, she says, "Of course, my darling."
2. The SG rings.

1:35 a.m.

I'll just leave it at that. I won't go into the nose business (less of it and more sticky up) or breast reduction requests, otherwise I will be here all night and Buddha may think I am a cheeky new Buddhist and that I'm only believing to get things.

Tuesday July 20th
10:00 a.m.

My room... soon to be a shrine to Buddha. Unless God gets his act together. Birds tweeting like birds at a bird party. Lovely sunny day. For some. I can see the sunshine glancing off Mr Next Door's bald head. He's playing with his stupid yappy little squirt dogs. Just a minute, I've spotted Angus hanging about in the potting shed area. Uh-oh, he looks a bit on the peckish side, like he fancies a poodle sandwich. I'd better go waggle a sausage at him and thereby avert a police incident.

How in the name of Mr Next Door's gigantic shorts am I supposed to be a Buddhist with these constant interruptions? I bet the Dalai Lama hasn't got a cat. Or a dad in New Zealand. (I wonder if the Dalai Lama's father is called the Daddy Lama?... I amaze myself sometimes because even though my life is a facsimile of a sham I can still laugh and joke!!)

10:36 a.m.
What is the point? Mum just laughed when I told her about looking after the house and told me to go and pack.

Midday
Even though it is quite obvious I am really depressed and in bed Mum comes poking around being all efficient and acting as if life is not a tragedy of a sham (which it is). She made me get up and show her what I had packed for Whangamata. She went ballisticisimus. "*Men are from Mars, Women are from Venus*, eyelash curlers, two bikinis and a cardigan?!"

"Well I won't be going out anywhere as I don't like sheep and my heart is broken."

"But you might wear your bikini?"

"I've only packed that for health reasons."

"What health reasons?"

"Well, if I can't eat anything because of my heartache, the

sun's rays may keep me from getting rickets. We did it in biology."

"It's winter over there."

"Typical."

"You are being ridiculous."

That's when all the pain came raging out of me. "I'm being ridiculous!!??? I'm being ridiculous??? I'm not the one who is dragging someone off to the other side of the world for NO good reason!!"

She went all red. "No good reason?! It's to see your dad!"

"I rest my case."

"Georgia, you are being horrible!" And she stormed off.

I feel a bit like crying. It's not my fault if I am horrible. I am under pressure. Why can't Dad be here? Then I could be horrible to him without feeling so horrible. (And without having to go to the other side of the planet. Most teenagers only have to go into the sitting room to be horrible to their dads.)

It's not easy having an absent dad, that's what people don't realise. I am effectively (apart from my mum and grandparents and my crap cousin James, etc.) an orphan.

1:00 p.m.

Libby crept into my room carrying a saucer of milk really carefully. She was on her tippy toes and purring. I said, "You are nice, Libbs. Just put it down; Angus is out hunting."

She very slowly and on tippy toes brought the saucer over to me and put it on my desk. She put her little hands on my head and started stroking my hair. My eyes filled up with tears. I said, "If I can't be happy in my life I can try and see that you have a nice life, Libbs. I will give up all thoughts of happiness myself and be like your Buddhist nurse. For your sake I will wear flat shoes and those really horrible orange robes and..."

Then Libby started pushing my head quite roughly down towards the saucer of milk. "C'mon, Ginger, come on. Milky pops."

She'll make me sleep in a cat basket soon. Honestly, I think it's about time she started kindergarten and mixed with normal children.

It takes twenty-four hours to fly to New Zealand.

6:00 p.m.

Uncle Eddie roared up on his pre-war motorbike. He's come round to collect Angus. How can I live without the huge furry fool? How can he live without me? No one else knows his special little ways. Who else will know that he likes you to trail his sausages around on a string so that he can pounce on them from behind the curtains? Who else will know about mouse racing? Not Uncle Eddie, that's for sure. He truly does come from Planet Bonkers. He came in wearing his motorbike leathers, took off his helmet and said, "How're you diddling?"

What is the matter with him? Why Mum thinks anyone as bald and barmy as him could look after an animal I don't know. Anyway, it's irrelevant what anyone thinks as he will never in a zillion years catch Angus and get him in a basket.

6:30 p.m.

I don't think I could be more sad. We are going to be away for months. I will miss all my friends; I'll lose the SG. My hockey career will be in ruins. Everyone knows the Maoris don't play hockey. They play... er... anyway, we haven't done New Zealand in geoggers yet, so I don't know what they do. Who cares?

31

6:35 p.m.

Time ticking away. It's like waiting to be buried, I should think. Or being in RE.

Phoned Jas. I wanted to know if Tom had heard anything from his gorgeous older brother, the Sex God, but I didn't want to let Jas know that I wasn't interested in her life. So I asked her a few questions about her "boyfriend" first.

"Hi, Jas, how are you and Tom getting along?"

She went all girlish and giggly. "Well, do you know, we were just laughing so much because Tom said that he was in the shop the other day and—"

"Jas, did he mention anything, you know, interesting?"

"Oh yeah, loads."

There was a pause – she drives me INSANE!

I said, "Like what?"

"Well, he was thinking of suggesting that they start selling more dairy products in their shop, because—"

"No, no, Jas I said interesting – not really, really boring. Has he, for instance, mentioned his gorgey older brother?"

Jas was a bit huffy but she said, "Hang on a minute." Then I heard her shouting, "Tom! Have you spoken to Robbie?"

In the distance I heard Tom shouting, "No, he's gone away on a footie trip."

I said to Jas, "I know that."

Jas shouted again, "She knows that."

Tom shouted, "Who knows that?"

"Georgia."

Then I heard Jas's mum shouting from somewhere, "Why does Georgia want to know about Robbie? Isn't she off to New Zealand?"

Jas shouted, "Yes, she is. But she's desperate to see him before she goes."

I said to Jas urgently, "Jas, Jas, I wanted to find out when he's back, I didn't want to discuss it with your street."

Jas went all huffy. "I'm only trying to help."

"Well don't."

"Well I won't, then."

"Good."

There was a silence. "Jas?"

"What?"

"What are you doing?"

"I'm not helping."

I'm going to have to kill her.

"Ask Tom when Robbie is due back."

"Huh. I don't see why I should, but I will."

She shouted out again, "Tom, when is Robbie back?"

Jas's mum yelled, "I thought he was going out with Lindsay?"

Tom yelled back, "He was, but then Georgia and him got together instead."

Jas's mum said, "Well, Lindsay will be very upset."

This was UNBELIEVABLE.

Tom yelled back again, "Tell Georgia he's not back again until late Monday."

Next Monday! Next Monday. By that time I would be being bored half to death by Maoris. I tried to be brave so that I wouldn't upset Jas. "I know I can joke about it and everything, but I have fancied Robbie for so long. And it's not just because he is in The Stiff Dylans. You know that. It's a whole year since I started stalking him. It was so groovy when he kissed me, I thought I would go completely jelloid and start dribbling. Luckily I didn't. And I think he will forget about that chunk of my hair snapping off, don't you?"

There was this clanking noise and then Jas said, with her mouth full, "Hello? Hello? What were you saying? I just went and got myself a sandwich while Tom was shouting at you."

Qu'est ce que le point?

7:30 p.m.

I can't believe Jas. She is dead to me. Like in the *Bible*, when somebody goes off and becomes a prostitute or something. She is now the girl who has no name.

9:00 p.m.

Phone rang. I leaped downstairs.

It was Rosie, Ellen, Jools and She Who Has No Name (Jas) calling me from the phone box at the end of our road. Rosie said in a fake Chinese accent, "Bringey selfey to phone boxey."

I put on some mascara and lippy so that no one would know about my broken heart. Not that it made the slightest difference to Mutti and Uncle Eddie – they were too busy trying to trap Angus.

He's lurking on top of my wardrobe. I know he's got a few snacks with him because he dropped a piece of mackerel on my head when I passed. He'll be happy up there for hours. Serve them right if they can't find him. Catnappers!

I don't want to be rude to the afflicted but Uncle Eddie is bald in a way which is the baldest I have ever seen. He looks like a boiled egg in leather trousers. Once he came round and after he and Mum had had their usual vat of wine he fell asleep in the back garden face down. So I drew another face on the back of his head. Very, very funny indeed, especially as I did it in indelible pen. He got his own back, though, by turning up to a school dance on his pre-war motorbike and asking all my mates where I was because he was my new boyfriend.

Still, that is life for you... one minute you are snogging a Sex God and have got up to number six on the snogging scale without crashing teeth. The next minute you are made to go to the other side of the world and hand out with Kiwi-a-gogos. Whose idea of a great time is to sit in mud pools and eat toasted maggots. (This is very, very true as I have been reading a brochure about Kiwi-a-gogo land and it says it in there.) Oh pig's bum!! Or as our tiny French friends say, *Le gran* bum *de le* porker!!!

9:30 p.m.
When I got to the phone box the gang were all in there. They squeezed open the door and Jools said, "*Bonsoir, ma petite* nincompoop."

Once I was in we were all squashed up like sardines at a fish party. Rosie managed to get a hand free and give me one of those photobooth photographs.

"We brought you a present to remember us by."

It was a picture of her, Jools, Ellen and Jas (She Who Has No Name), only they had their noses stuck back at the tip with Sellotape so that it made them look like pigs with hair.

On the back it said, GRUNTINGS from your mates. STY in touch. This is a PIGTURE to remember us by.

It made me a bit tearful, but I put on a brave face. "Cheers, thanks a lot. Goodnight."

We had to get out of the telephone box because Mark (the boy from up the road with the enormous gob who I went out with for a fortnight but dumped me because this other girl Ella let him "do things to her") came to use the phone. He just looked at us as we all struggled out. He really has got the biggest mouth I have ever seen. I was lucky to escape from snogging him with my face still in one piece.

BG (Big Gob) said, "All right?" in a way which meant, "All right, you lesbians?"

What do I care, though? My life is over anyway.

We all walked back to my house arm in arm. I wouldn't link up with Jas though because she has annoyed me. Uncle Eddie must have eventually got Angus into the cat basket because the gardening gloves he was wearing were lying in the driveway with the thumbs torn off.

We all hugged and cried. It was awful. I'd nearly got to the door when Jas sort of threw herself at me. She couldn't speak because she was crying so much and she said, "Georgia, nothing will be the same without you... I... I love you. I'm sorry I ate my sandwich."

Wednesday July 21st
Dawn — well, 10:00 a.m.

Phoned my dearest friend Jas who loves me. Huh.

Now that she thinks she has got a "proper" boyfriend she acts like she is one hundred and eighty.

"Look, Gee-gee, I can't talk really because I am on the dash to meet Tom. Dig you later, though. *Ciao* for now."

...*Ciao* for now? I wonder if she has finally snapped? Nobody really cares about me. No one wants you when you are in trouble; no one is interested when you are not the life and soul of the party. I may have to try to make it up with God again at this rate.

38

2:30 p.m.

I don't care what happens. I am not going to New Zealand. Not. Definitely. They will have to carry me on to the plane. Or give me knock-out drugs.

That is it. I am not going.

3:00 p.m.

I am not speaking to Mum but as she has gone out shopping (again) she probably hasn't noticed.

3:19 p.m.

Sitting by the phone and using telepathy to make it ring. I've read about it a lot – it's where you use your willpower to make something happen. In my head I was saying, "Ring, phone!" and "The phone will ring and it will be Robbie... by the time I count to ten."

3:21 p.m.

"OK, the phone will ring and it will be Robbie by the time I count to a hundred..."

3:30 p.m.

"...in French. By the time I count to one hundred in French the phone will ring and it will be SG." (God, or whoever it is that deals with willpower, will respect that I am making a bloody huge effort by counting in a foreign language.)

Everything really is sheer desperadoes and in tins. In two days' time I will be on the other side of the world and the Sex God will be on this side of the world. And, what is more, I will be a day ahead of him. And upside down.

3:39 p.m.

I've got an appalling headache now.

While we are on the subject of French, why in the name of Louise the Fourteenth did Madame Slack (honestly – that is her name) make us learn a song called "*Mon Merle a Perdu une Plume*"?

My blackbird has lost a feather. That will be a great boon and help if I ever get to go to Paris. I won't be able to get a sandwich for love nor money but I will be able to chat to *le* French about my blackbird's feathers. Not that I have got a blackbird and, if I did have one, believe me it wouldn't be just the one feather it would lose with Angus around. Not that he is around.

I really miss him already. He is the best cat anyone ever had. I can still imagine his furry head snuggled up in my bed. Bits of feather round his mouth. The way he used to bring me little presents. A vole, or a bit of poodle ear or something.

3:41 p.m.
How do you say my blackbird has had its legs chewed off by my cat? *Mon merle a perdu les jambes...*

Phone rang
3:45 p.m.
Thank goodness, because I thought I was going to have to count up to a hundred in German and nobody wants that. (And besides, I can't.)

"It's me, Jas."

"Oh... What do YOU want?"

"I've just called to see how you are."

I said, "Dead actually, I died a few hours ago. Goodbye."

That will teach her. I'm not going to answer the phone if she rings back, either.

5:00 p.m.

She didn't ring back. Typical.

My room
In bed
10:30 p.m.

Mum and Libby came back in. When they popped their heads round my door I pretended to be asleep. Libby crept over quietly – well, her idea of creeping quietly, which is the loudest thing I have ever heard.

Mum whispered, "Give you big sister a kiss, Libbs, because she's upset."

Then I felt this wet thing sucking on the end of my nose. I shot up in bed. I said, "Does anyone else's sister kiss like that? Why is she so obsessed with my nose?"

11:15 p.m.

After the nose-sucking incident I am as awake as two awake things. Just gazing out of my bedroom window into the dark night. When you gaze at the stars it makes you feel really small. We have been discussing infinity in Physics: you know, how there is no end to the universe, and so on. Herr Kamyer said there might even be a parallel universe to the one we live on somewhere out there. There might be another Georgia Nicolson sitting in her bedroom, thinking, What on earth is the point?

11:17 p.m.
Another Georgia Nicolson who is being forced to leave a Sex God and all her mates (and this does not include Jas). To go to the other side of the world. Double *merde*.

11:29 p.m.
I've just had a horrible thought. If there is a parallel me, there will be a parallel Wet Lindsay. And a parallel Nauseating P. Green. And two pairs of Mr Next Door's shorts. Good grief.

Thursday July 22nd
Day before the last day of my life
Hunger protest
2:00 p.m.
Even though it is quite obvious even to the VERY dim that I am not eating, Mum hasn't noticed. She said, "Do you want some oven chips and beans?"

43

And I said, "I will never eat again."

She just said, "OK," and tucked in with Libbs.

I had to creep into the kitchen and finish off the chips she had left.

4:00 p.m.

In my room. Practising feeling lonely and friendless in preparation for the months ahead.

4:05 p.m.

I haven't heard from my so-called mates for days. Well, since this morning, anyway. I don't need to practise. I AM lonely and friendless.

4:10 p.m.

I went into the front room to watch TV. Libby was snoozing but woke up when I sat down. She stood up on her little fat legs and put her arms up to me.

"I love my Georgie, I lobe my Georgie."

She made it into a little song:

"Haha, I lobe my Georgie,

I love my little Girgie,

Gingie, Gingie.

Hahahaha. Ginger, I love Ginger... my Ginger."

In her tiny mad brain I am half cat, half sister. I picked her up and we snuggled down on the sofa together. At least I have someone who loves me in this family, even if she is bonkers.

Mum came in and said, "You look really sweet together. It only seems a little while ago that you were that size, Georgie. Dad and I used to take you to the park and you used to have a little hat with earflaps that were like cats' paws. You were such a sweet little girl."

Oh good Lord, here we go. It will be, "How did my little girl get so big...?"

Sure enough, Mum's eyes got all watery and she started stroking my hair (very annoying) and doing the "How did my little Georgie get so..." routine.

Fortunately (or unfortunately, depending on where you were sitting) Libby let off the smelliest, loudest fart known to humanity. It came out of her bum-oley with such force that she lifted off my knee – like a hovercraft. Even she looked surprised by what had come out of her.

I pushed her off my knee and leaped up. "Libby, that is disgusting!!!! I blame you, Mum, for the bean extravaganza.

It's not natural, the amount of stuff that comes out of such a little girl."

Phwoaar...

Grandad farted once when we were out in the street. Really loudly. When he looked around behind him there was a woman walking her dachshund dog. You know, those little sausage dog things. The woman heard Grandad's fart (who didn't?) and she said, "Well, really!!"

And Grandad said, "I'm terribly sorry, madam, I seem to have shot the legs off your dog." Which was possibly the last semi-sane thing he said. I'd still rather stay here with him than go to Kiwi-a-gogo.

I said to Mum, "Well, can I go and live with Grandad, then?"

And she said, "He lives in an old people's home."

And I said, "So?"

But she is so mad and unreasonable she wouldn't even discuss it.

11:30 p.m.

All my mates came and did a candlelit vigil underneath my bedroom window. Sven wore a paper hat. I don't know why.

Does it matter? It was just his Swedish way of saying goodbye. They all sang *"Mon Merle a Perdu une Plume"* as a tribute. Well, they sang the first verse before Mr and Mrs Next Door came and complained that they were frightening their dogs. Jas said, "I'm going to stay silently here all night."

But then Sven said, "Chips, now." And they all went off.

It was so sad.

Friday July 23rd
The day the world ends
Midday

Decided to have to be dragged out of bed by the police so that the world will know how I have been treated. I have tied myself to the bedhead with my dressing-gown sleeves. I can imagine the newspaper headlines: Promising hockey superstar teenager fights attempts to force her to Kiwi-a-gogo land. I've put on a hint of make-up just in case, for the photos.

12:10 p.m.

Mum surprised me by bursting into my room all flushed like a pancake.

"Guess what?!!!! We're not going to New Zealand because your dad is coming home!!!!!"

I said, "What?"

She was hugging me and didn't seem to notice I was like a rigid hamster in bed.

I was a bit dazed. "Vati, home, coming?"

Great news!!!!!!!!!
1:00 p.m.

My dad has had his shoes blown off by a rogue bore!!!!! All this hot steam shot out of something he was fixing and he leaped off and broke his foot. Mum has put her foot down with a firm hand and said she will not take her children to a place where steam shoots out of the ground.

She said to me, "It's hard enough getting you to get out of bed as it is, I'm not giving you more excuses." Which is incredibly unfair, but I didn't say anything, because inside I was saying "Yessssss!!!!!!"

The only fly in the manger is that Vati is going to be coming home when his contract is finished. Still, if it is a choice of going to live in Kiwi-a-gogo land or having to put up with Vati snooping around my bedroom and telling me what it was like in the seventies, I suppose I will choose having the grumpy moustachioed one.

Mum is hideously happy. She won't stop hugging me. Which I think is on the hypocritical side but I didn't say anything. I just hugged her back and asked her quickly for a fiver. Which she gave me. Yesss!!!!

Beautiful English summer's day. Lovely, lovely drizzly rain!!! We don't have to go to Kiwi-a-gogo!!!

Thank you, God. I will always believe in you. I was only pretending to become a Buddhist.

3:00 p.m.
I put on some really loud music in my room and started to unpack my bikini. Lalalalala... fabbity fab fab. Marvy and double cool with knobs.

Uncle Eddie turned up with a bottle of champagne and Angus in a basket. I noticed Uncle Eddie had put a muzzle on him. What a week. Angus soon had it off and I could see him strolling around his domain. (The dustbins.) When I went downstairs Uncle Eddie had picked up Libby and was dancing around with her. She was singing, "Uncle Eggy, Uncle Eggy," which is quite funny when you think about it.

4:20 p.m.

My little room. I love you, my little room!!! Lalalalalalala. Fabbity fab fab. Ho-di-hum. Everything is so lovely: my little Reeves and Mortimer poster with them in the nuddy-pants, my little desk, my little bed... my little window overlooking next door's garden.

5:00 p.m.

Phoned the Ace Crew and they went mental. Just put the phone down when there was a ring on the doorbell. It was Mr Next Door. His glasses were on all sideways. He did not say, "I am so glad you are not going, Georgia." In fact, he didn't say anything but just handed over a sweeping brush and stomped off.

Attached to the bottom part of the brush was Angus. He dragged the brush into the kitchen. There was the sound of pots and pans and chairs crashing over. I called out, "Libbs, Angus is back."

11:00 p.m.

Before I went up to bed I looked into the kitchen. Libbs was feeding Angus cat food by hand. Aaahhh, this was more like it!! Back to normal.

Saturday July 24th

11:00 a.m.

Summer. Birds tweeting. Voles voleing. Poodles poodling. I notice that we have new neighbours across the road. I hope they are a bit more considerate than Mr and Mrs Mad who used to live there.

Oh, they've got a cat! It looks like one of those pedigree Burmese ones, all leaping around. In a sort of fenced enclosure. They are very expensive, pedigree Burmese cats. They are the Naomi Campbells of the cat world. Not that they do a lot of modelling. Too furry. And not tall enough. Although they would be really good on the catwalk!!! Hahahahaha. Lalalalala. I think I am a comedy genius. Now if only the SG would phone and say, "I'm coming round now, oh gorgeous one. I didn't realise how close I came to losing you. I am mesmerised by your beautosity." Life would be beyond fab and entering the marvy zone.

Midday

Met Jas and we went to the park. I've got a spot on my chin but I've made it look like a beauty spot with an eyebrow pencil. With my shades on I look a bit like an Italian person.

I think Jas was embarrassed about me not going to NZ after what she said. I am too considerate to mention it so I just said, "Do you really love me, Jas?"

She went all red.

As we strolled by the tennis courts we saw Melanie Griffiths sunbathing. I may have mentioned this before but she has got the largest breasts known to humanity. Some lads went by and went "Phwooar!". One of them pretended to be juggling. Sometimes I feel that boys will always remain a mystery to me. I've felt that particularly since BG from up the road rested his hand on my basooma for no particular reason. Mel saw us looking so I said, "Oh, hi Mel!" sincerely.

She said, "Hi!" but I don't think she meant it.

I said to Jas, "Where does she get her bras from? They must be made by those blokes who built the Forth Bridge, Ted and Mick Forth." I just made that up; I don't know what they were called.

We lay down on the grass to sunbathe and Jas said, "Do you think I should get a bra?"

I was thinking what I should wear when I saw Robbie again. I said, "Robbie hasn't phone yet, you know."

Jas was silent. I squinted round at her and she was sort of

wobbling her shoulders around. I said, "What in the name of pantyhose are you doing?"

She said, "I'm seeing if my basoomas wobble."

Jas can be spectacularly dim. I think that if I dressed Angus in her school uniform probably no one would notice for days. Unless they tried to take a snack away.

I said, "Do the pencil test. You put a pencil under a breast and if it falls out you are OK. If it stays there, sort of trapped by your basooma, you're not and you should get help and support in the bra department."

She was full-on, attention-wise, then. "Really?"

"Yeah. Sadly my mum can get a whole pencil case up there."

Jas was rummaging about. "I've got a pencil in my rucky, I'm going to try it."

"Jas, Tom hasn't said anything about Robbie, has he?"

As per usual Jas had gone off into the twilight world in her head. She was fiddling about with a pencil up her T-shirt. She said, "Hahahahaha, it fell out!!! I passed, I passed... you try it."

I wasn't interested. "Why would SG snog me and say 'see you later' if he didn't mean 'see you later'? Do you think he's worried about me being younger than him? Or do you think it's my nose?"

You might as well be talking to a duck. Jas was shoving the pencil at me. "Go on, go on... you're scared."

"Try it, then."

"No I'm not. I'm not frightened of a pencil."

"Oh for goodness' sake."

I grabbed the pencil from her and pulled up my top and put the pencil underneath my right basooma. Actually it stuck there, but I jiggled a bit. I said, "Yeah, it falls out."

Jas said, "You jiggled."

"I did not."

"You did. I saw you."

"I didn't. You're a mad biscuit."

"You did. Look, let me do it, I'll show you."

She grabbed the pencil and was trying to put it under my basooma when Jackie and Alison, the Bummer Twins, came round the corner of the tennis courts. Jackie removed the fag from her mouth long enough to say, "Well, well, well, our lezzo friends are out for an afternoon fondle."

Oh no, here we go again with the lesbian rumours. That will be something to look forward to next term.

Monday July 26th
2:00 p.m.

Phew, what a scorcher!!! Sun shining, birds tweeting. Mr and Mrs Next Door in their garden. They are wearing shorts – again. Mr Next Door's shorts really are gigantic in the bottom department. You'd think that out of courtesy to others he'd keep out of public view when he was wearing them. What if a very, very old person – even older than him – came along unexpectedly? And what if they weren't in peak medical condition? The sight of Mr Next Door in his shorts could bring on a dangerous spasm. Still, that is another example of the bottomless (oo-er!) selfishosity of so-called grown-ups for you.

Teatime
4:50 p.m.

Fabulous day... not. Grandad came round. Even he was wearing shorts. As I said to Mum, "There is really no need for that."

He is so bow-legged that Angus can walk in between his legs with a stick and Grandad doesn't even notice. Mind you he doesn't notice much as he lives in the twilight world of the elderly mad. After fiddling in his prehistoric shorts he gave me twenty pence and said, "There you are, don't spend it all at once." Then he laughed so much his false teeth shot out. He was wheezing away for so long I thought he'd choke to death and then I'd have to do the Heimlich manoeuvre. Miss Stamp (Sports Kommandant) made us learn it in First Aid. If someone swallows a boiled sweet or something and chokes, you grab them from behind and put your arms round below their breastbone. Then you squeeze them really hard until the sweet shoots out. Apparently some German bloke called Mr Heimlich made it up. Why Germans have to go round grabbing people innocently choking on sweets I don't know. But they do. That is the mystery of the German people.

8:00 p.m.
Well, that is it. No call from the SG. He must be back. I can't call him because I have pride. Well actually, I did phone him but there was no reply. I didn't leave a message. I don't understand boys. How could you do number six type snogging and then not call someone?

8:10 p.m.
Buddhism is the only way. I must meditate and be calm.

My room
8:20 p.m.

I found one of Mum's kaftans that she got when she went to India on the hippie trail. She has some very sad photos of her and Dad with hilarious haircuts in Katmandu. Dad looks like he has got a big nappy on. She gets the photos out when she is drunk, especially if you beg her not to.

I put on the kaftan and was listening to some dolphins on a meditation tape. It was called "Peaceful Universe". Squeak, squeak, squeak. On and on – it would go quiet for a bit and then squeak, squeak, squeak. If dolphins are so intelligent why don't they learn to speak properly? Instead of squeaking? It is fantastically irritating. I would turn it off but I am too depressed to get off the bed.

8:40 p.m.

Phone rings. Of course, everyone else is far too busy to answer it. So I'll tramp all the way downstairs and get it.

I yelled out, "Don't worry, Mum, I'll come all the way down and answer the phone which is probably for you. You try and get some rest!"

Mum shouted from the living room, "OK, thanks."

I picked up the receiver. "Yes?"

It was Robbie!!! Yes and treble fabuloso!! He's got such a lovely voice; quite deep – not quite as deep as Grandad's, but then he doesn't smoke forty cigarettes a minute. He said he'd been away.

I was thinking, I know you have, you great huge sexy hunk!!! My lips are stiff with puckering!!! But I didn't say that, I said, "Oh, have you?" which I thought was quite cool and alluring. Anyway, the short and short of it is that he's really, really glad that I didn't go to Kiwi-a-gogo and I'm going round to his place tomorrow!!! His parents have gone away.

Ooooooohhhhhh. I'm all shakey and nervous now. I'm like a cat on a hot tin roof. We did *Cat On a Hot Tin Roof* in English. There was no cat in it... or a tin roof... or... stop it, brain, stop it!!!!

8:45 p.m.
Phoned Jas.

"He called me!!"

"Who?"

It's like talking to a sock. "Jas. HE called me. HE – the one and only HE in the universe."

Jas came round to discuss what I should wear. We went up to my room. Unfortunately I forgot to warn Jas about the hammock that Libby had made for her dolls. She'd made it out of one of Mum's commodious bras and tied it across the landing. Jas grazed her shins quite badly when she fell over. She was going, "Ow, ow!", but I can't be bothered with minor injuries just now.

She hobbled into my room and we looked through my wardrobe. I held things up and Jas went, "No. No. Maybe. No, too tarty. No, no... er... maybe."

I was trying on a suede mini and she said, "Erlack!! The front of your legs are quite hairy but the backs of your legs are all baldy."

I had a look. She was right!!! Time for operation smoothy legs. I grumbled to her as we went down to the bathroom. "What is the point of evolution? Why bother giving us hairy front legs and baldy back legs? When can that ever have been useful in our fight for survival?"

Jas said, "Perhaps it was to frighten things off."

I said, "Oh yeah, that will be it. Stone Age girl would have said, 'Here comes a big dinosaur chasing me from behind. It thinks I am a push-over because of my baldy legs, but wait till I turn round! I'll scare off the big lug with my terrifying hairy front legs.' That will be the explanation."

Jas wasn't interested in my scientosity because she was looking through the bathroom cabinet. "Your mum has got loads of anti-ageing creams, hasn't she?"

"I know. It's sad. Why doesn't she save all that money and put it towards some new spectacles or a hat? Or a decent bra that can contain her gigantic basoomas."

9:30 p.m.

Mum's hair remover worked a treat; my legs were smoothy smooth. I was tempted to use a bit on my eyebrows but I remembered the last time I had shaved them and they had taken two weeks to grow back.

Clothes-wise we decided on a turtle-necked crop top (implies that I am mature for my years, on the brink of womanhood, etc... but doesn't go as far as saying "I am desperate for a snog"). In the leg department it was the tight Capri trousers.

Jas said, "Tom is going away on work experience this term. I will be on my own for weeks. I'll really miss him. Do you know, he said the other day that he..."

In a caring way I said, "Go home now, Jas, I have to get my beauty sleep."

11:00 p.m.
In bed nice and early. I've barricaded my door so that Angus and Libby can't get in.

Midnight
I am SO nervous... What if I have forgotten how to snog? What if all my snogging lessons go out of my mind at the last minute and we bump teeth?

1:00 a.m.
Or I lose my grip altogether and go to the same side with my head as he is going, and knock him out? Heeeeelp!!!!

What if I have one of those laughing fits that you can't stop? You know, when you remember something... like for instance when Herr Kamyer took us on a school trip and when we arrived at the railway station he said, "Ach yes, here ve are!" and then opened the door on the wrong side of the train and fell out of the carriage.

Hahahahahahahaha... hahahahaa. You see, I'm doing it

now. I'm laughing by myself in the middle of the night in my room.

OhmyGodohmyGodohmyGod. Hahahahahahahahaha.

Tuesday July 27th
SG Day
Setting off to his house.
7:00 p.m.

It's taken most of the day to achieve my natural make-up look. Just a subtle touch to enhance my natural beauty(!). I wanted the just-tumbled-out-of-bed look, so I only used undercover concealer, foundation, hint of bronzer, eye pencil, eight layers of mascara, lip liner, lippy and lip-gloss, and I left it at that.

7:20 p.m.

Jas phoned to wish me luck. She said, "Tell me all about it when you get home. Remember what number you get up to on the snogging scale. Are you wearing a bra? I think it would be wise because you don't want to wobble all over the place."

I said, "Goodbye, Jas."

I'm not wearing a bra; I thought I would go free and akimbo. I just won't make any sudden movements.

Walking down Arundel Street
7:30 p.m.

Brrr, not quite as warm and bright as it was earlier. A bit overcast, actually, and... oh no... it's starting to rain! It's too far to go back home for an umby... it will probably stop in a minute.

7:40 p.m.

Outside Robbie's gate. It really is raining quite hard now. I'm wet through and really cold. I think my trousers have shrunk; they are hugging my bottom in a vice-like grip. I wonder if I look all right?

I'll nip into the telephone box opposite his house and check my mirror.

In the telephone box
7:45 p.m.

My trousers have shrunk so tight around my bottom that I can't bend my legs. This is hopeless. Brrr. Why is everything going wrong? I can't go to see the Sex God looking like this. I'll have to phone him up and say I'm ill.

7:50 p.m.

SG answered the phone, "Hello."

Swoon swoon.

I said, "Roggie, nit's ne, Neorgia."

"What's wrong with your voice?"

"Der nl'd gat a trrible cold nd Im nin bed."

"Do they have beds in telephone boxes?"

"Dnno."

"Georgia, I can see you through the window."

When I looked across at his house, he waved at me. Oh GODDDDDD!!!!!!

He said, "Come over."

What can I do, what can I do? My top is all wet. And there are two bumpy things in it. Great! It looks like I've got two peas down the front of my top. Typical, the only thing Mum has ever ironed for me and she has ironed it wrong.

As I walked up to the door I tried to flatten out the bumpy bits. But it wasn't my top sticking up... it was ME!!! My nipples!!!!! What were they doing?!!! Why were they sticking out? I hadn't told them to do that. How could I get them back in again? I'd have to cross my arms in a casual way and hope he didn't offer me a cup of coffee.

7:55 p.m.

The back door opened and there he was!! The Sex God had landed. I went even more jelloid. He was so gorgey... so... oooooh and er and yum yum and scrumbos and yummy scrumbos. His hair was all floppy, he had on dark jeans and a white T-shirt and you could see his shoulders (one on each side). He's got really, really dark blue eyes and long dark eyelashes and a big mouth, sort of soft looking. He's not a girlie boy though, he's definitely a boyie boy, which I think is handy in a boy myself.

Midnight

I love him, I love him. I love you, Robbie, oh yes I do. When I'm not near you I'm blue... What else rhymes with Robbie? Gobbie? Snoggie? Knobbie?

12:30 a.m.

I can't sleep, life is too brilliant. I may never sleep again.

It was such a fab night. We talked for a bit – well, I said, "My dad had his shoes blown off by a rogue bore," and he said, "Does anything normal ever happen to you?" Which I took as a compliment.

He played me a song on his guitar. I didn't really know what to do when he did that. I just sat on the sofa next to him with an attractive half-smile on my face and my arms crossed). It was quite a long song and by the end of it my cheeks ached like billio. In fact, I think I might have cheek strain. I tried to keep my nose sucked in at the same time; I didn't want it wandering across my face.

He told me that he is going to go to university to do music properly. I said, "I'm going to be a vet." I don't know why as I'm not. I didn't seem to be able to make anything come out of my mouth that had anything to do with my brain. He looked into my eyes and went quiet, and I went quiet and looked back at him. I tried not to blink. That seemed to go on for about a million years. In the end I had a sort of nervy spasm and went and looked at a photograph of a dog that was on a table. He probably thinks I am obsessed with animals as I am a trainee vet (not).

He came over and put his arm round my shoulder. I had an overwhelming urge to start doing Cossack dancing as a very funny joke, but just in time I remembered that boys don't like girls for jokes. Then he kissed me. I think he may be the best snogger in the universe. Although I have only snogged two other boys so far, and one of those was part boy part whelk, so I can't be entirely sure. SG does that varying pressure thing that Rosie says foreign boys do. You know, soft and then hard and then medium and then hard again. I could have quite literally snogged until the cows came home. And when they came home I would have shouted, "WHAT HAVE YOU COWS COME HOME FOR? CAN'T YOU SEE I'M SNOGGING, YOU STUPID HERBIVORES???"

I think I may be a bit feverish.

1:30 a.m.

I am going to be nice to everyone from now on. Even Wet Lindsay, Robbie's ex. I won't say to her, "Yesssssss!!!!" I will be grown-up and nice.

The only fly in the landscape is that when he walked me to my gate and said goodnight he tweaked my nose. And he said, "I'll see you later."

1:35 a.m.

What does that mean? Not the "see you later" bit, because no one knows what that means. I mean the tweaking the nose business.

1:40 a.m.

Does it mean, "Hey, you adorable cute thing," or does it mean, "Cor, what a size that conk is, I wonder if I can get all of it in one hand?"

Wednesday July 28th
3:35 p.m.

I am a Sex God's girlfriend. But I will not let it spoil my naturalness.

Phoned Jas: "Even when I have loads of interesting and glamorous friends I would still want to be friends with you. Because we are proper friends. We should never let boys come between us."

Jas said, "Tom is going to buy me one of those stick-on transfer tattoos. I'm going to put it on my bottom while he is away and not wash it off until he gets back."

"Jas, can you leave your bottom out of this? Please."

Friday July 30th
5:00 p.m.

Made my dear mutti and sister a meal today. Mashed potatoes and sausages. I thought Mum was going to cry.

10:00 p.m.

Early to bed, early to rise, makes a girl... er... anyway, it gets a girl out of the way of her mutti who had a nervy b. when she saw the state of the kitchen.

10:15 p.m.

Why do I always get the blame for every little thing? Is it really my fault that a couple of pans caught fire? I put them out.

Still, I refuse to be upset. I will remain calm beneath my egg and olive oil face mask.

Saturday July 31st
7:55 p.m.

Dreamy dreamy, smiley smiley.

However no phone calley. Never mindey.

Snogging Withdrawal

Sunday August 1st

8:00 a.m.

I've persuaded Jas to come to church with me to thank God for making Dad have his shoes blown off and also for giving me a Sex God as a plaything.

10:00 a.m.

When I got round to Jas's house she was sitting on her wall in the shortest skirt known to humanity. When I wear skirts like that my grandad says, "You can see what you had for your dinner." I don't know what on earth he is talking about but then neither does anyone else, except probably dogs.

Jas leaped off the wall. Her skirt was about four centimetres long.

I said, "Is it a long time since you went to church, Jas?" and she said, "It's OK, I'm wearing really big knickers."

Church
10:40 a.m.

Good grief. Now I know why I don't go to church much. It is not what is generally known as Fun City Arizona. I was forced to sing "All Things Bright and Beautiful" which is bad enough, but there was a further treat in store. The vicar, ("Call me Arnold") tries to be "modern". So to really get "with it" Call me Arnold had got some absolute saddos to play guitars as an accompaniment. One of the boys on guitar was called Norman and as if that is not cruel enough he had acne. And not just ordinary acne, he had acne of the entire head.

But as we left I remembered that I was supposed to be being grateful so I said, "Sorry about Spotty Norman, God, I will be nice to him next time I see him," (inwardly) and put a pound in the collection box.

Monday August 2nd
12:10 p.m.

Still no news from the SG. I've been going to bed really early to make the hours pass more quickly.

I tried snogging the back of my hand to stave off snogging withdrawal but it's no good.

3:30 p.m.

Cor phew... boiling again. The sun was shining like a great big fried egg. Jas and Jools and Ellen and me went sunbathing in the park. I took off my shades and got the shock of my life: in the sunshine my legs looked like Herr Kamyer's legs. They were all pale-looking. Not as hairy or German as his legs, obviously.

I said, "Ellen, why are your legs so brown?"

She said, "Oh, I used some of that Kool Tan stuff."

Maybe the SG noticed my Herr Kamyer legs? I must get some Kool Tan.

Tuesday August 3rd
10:30 p.m.

When Jas came round for us to practise hairstyles I made her let me kiss the back of her calf to see if she could feel any teeth. She leaped about, going, "Erlack, erlack, get off, get off, it feels disgusting, like a sort of sucky Spotty Norman." Which is not very reassuring.

She said Tom touched her basooma the other night. In revenge I said, "How would he know it wasn't your shoulder?" She honestly does think she is like Kate Moss. It is very, very sad.

Midnight
SG didn't touch my basooma. I wonder if that is bad? Mind you, I had my arms folded for a lot of the time because of the nipple emergency.

Wednesday August 4th
4:00 p.m.
Phoned Jas.

"I'm really worried now. It's been over a week. I wonder if it is my nose? Perhaps SG only likes little sticky-up noses like Wet Lindsay's?"

Jas said, "Maybe a headband would help. You should make more of your forehead and that would take the emphasis away from your nose."

"At least I've got a forehead, not like Wet Lindsay who has got a tiny little forehead. In fact, she is really just hair and then eyebrows. How could the SG go out with someone with no forehead?"

"She's got quite nice legs."

"What do you mean? Nice – not like mine? Shut up, Jas."

"OK, keep your hair on."

"Nauseating P. Green, on the other hand, has got the HUGEST forehead known to humanity. In fact, she is a walking forehead in a frock. I must get away from this forehead business, it's making me feel a bit mad."

4:30 p.m.

In the bathroom experimenting with a headband. Hmmm, headband seems to emphasise my nose. In fact, it's like wearing a big notice on my head that says, "Hey, everyone!!! Look at my incredibly big schnozzle!!"

4:40 p.m.

While I had been doing headband work I hadn't been paying much attention to Libbs. She had come into the bathroom and got up on the lavatory seat. Her hair was all sticking up like a mad earwig but she won't let you comb it. I said, "Libby, things will start nesting in it," and she said, "Aaahh nice." Then she started going, "Bzzz, bzzz, bzzy bzz, bzz," like a mad bee.

I was experimenting with sucking in my nose to see if it made it look any smaller when Mum came barging in. (Not bothering to knock or anything.) Anyway, she went even more bananas than usual. Libby had put all of the loo paper down her knickers because she wanted to be a bumble bee. I'd heard her buzzing but I didn't pay any attention. Mum was all red-faced.

"Georgia, all you think about is how you bloody look. The house could burn down around you before you would stop looking in that mirror."

I raised my eyebrows ironically. Talk about the pot calling the other pot a black kettle, er... well whatever. She really has got a volatile temper; she should go to anger management classes. I will suggest it to her. But not just now as she has got a brush in her hand.

4:50 p.m.
My violent, bad-tempered mother has gone out. Nothing in the fridge. Oh, I tell a lie, there is a half-eaten sausage. Yum yum.

4:55 p.m.
Grandad said that as you get older gravity pulls on your nose and makes it bigger and bigger.

5:00 p.m.
Why couldn't I come from a decent gene bank? Nice, well-formed parents, like Jas's mum and dad. Nice and compact, nothing too sticky-outy. Instead I get massive "danger to shippings" from Mum and a massive conk from my dad. If Robbie doesn't like me it is Vati's fault. If it is true about the gravity business then Dad will need a wheelbarrow to carry his nose around in soon. Good, serve him right for ruining my life.

7:00 p.m.
I'm so hot and restless. Oh Robbie, where are you? My nose feels tremendously heavy.

8:00 p.m.
I put on a really loud record and danced about to get rid of my excess snogosity.

8:05 p.m.

When I looked in the mirror I could see my basoomas bobbling about. Good grief and *sacré bleu*!! They look like they are doing their own dance!

In Mum's Vanity Fair it says that all the posh type ladies go to a special woman behind Harrod's to get their bras properly fitted.

8:15 p.m.

The Queen must go there, then. Apparently this woman who does the bras is such an expert that she can just look at someone and say what size bra they should have. No suggestion of pencil cases. I wish I could go to her.

8:30 p.m.

When the Queen goes, this woman must just look at her and yell to her assistant, "Get the Queen a bra in size forty-eight D." Or whatever size the Queen is.

9:00 p.m.

The Queen is about five foot high, so if she was a size sixty D that would make her like a five-foot ball.

9.30 p.m.

I wish I didn't have that in my head.

Midnight

Should I call him? Oh I don't know what to do. I don't know what to do.

Thursday August 5th
Still boiling
4:00 p.m.

Jools, Ellen, Rosie, Jas and me went to town to try on make-up in Boots and Miss Selfridge. I cheered up a bit, especially as we did this limping thing on the way home. You link up and all limp together. And you're not allowed to break arms no matter what happens. This tremendously old bloke got shirty with us because we accidentally stampeded his Labrador. After that we went into the park and sat on the swings for a rest. Rosie said, "Oh I fancy a fag."

I was shocked. I said, "I didn't know you smoked."

And she said, "It's just to relax."

Rosie put a cigarette in her mouth and got out her lighter. We were all looking. Unfortunately she must have set the flame too high because when she flicked it a flame shot up about twelve centimetres and set fire to her fringe. We beat it out but the hair was all singed and short. She went home with her hand over her fringe. After she had gone the rest of us swang backwards and forwards for a few minutes.

I said, "Rosie smokes quite a lot, doesn't she?"

And then we all got the helpless laughing. You know, that laughing that makes your tummy hurt and makes you cry and gulp and choke? And you've laughed for long enough and you want to stop but you can't. Then you do stop and you think it's all right but then someone starts again. I just couldn't stop. And that's when I saw HIM. The Sex God. With his mates from The Stiff Dylans. He looked like he was coming across to say hello. And you know when you really, really should stop laughing because otherwise it will be really bad and everyone will hate you? But you can't? Well I had that.

10:00 p.m.
Rang Robbie. His mum said he was at rehearsal. Still he likes a laugh himself, so it will be all right.

♥ 79

Midnight

On the other hand I wasn't by any means doing my attractive half-smiling when he saw me. I had a look at myself in the mirror doing proper, unadulterated laughing, the kind of laughing where you just let your nose and mouth go free and wild.

12:15 a.m.

That is it, my life is over; I must go to the ugly home immediately.

Friday August 6th

11:00 a.m.

A letter arrived for me. From Robbie. My hands were shaking when I opened it.

11:30 a.m.

Back in bed. I CANNOT believe my life. It is beyond pooiness. It has gone well beyond the Valley of the Poo and entered the Galaxy of *Merde*.

11:45 a.m.

I re-read the letter from Robbie again. It still says the same thing though.

> Dear Georgia,
>
> I have been thinking and thinking about this. And although I think you are great, and I really do like you, well, I saw you with your mates yesterday having a laugh and you seemed so young. The facts are that I am seventeen, nearly eighteen, and if anyone knew I was even thinking about going out with a fourteen-year-old I would never hear the end of it. Where would we go for our dates? Youth club or something? You see what I mean, don't you?
>
> I think it is best we stay away from each other for a year or so. You need to see someone more your own age. My brother has a really nice mate called Dave. He's a good laugh. You'd like him.
>
> I'm really sorry.
> Love Robbie xxxxxxxxx

Midday

On the phone to Jas. I was shaking with rage.

Jas said, "Well, erm… if he's a good laugh, maybe you should meet him."

"Jas, are you really saying that I should just stop liking one person and start liking another one, just like that? What if I said, 'Hey, Jas, forget about Tom, why not go out with Spotty Norman? He's got a really great shaped head underneath the acne'?"

Saturday August 7th
6:20 p.m.

I hate him. I hate him.

On the phone to Jas.

"How dare he find another boyfriend for me? I hate him!!!"

Sunday August 8th
3:50 p.m.

That is absolutely it for me now. He can't treat me like that. I have my pride. How dare he question my maturiosity?

On the phone to Jas. "Jas?"

"What?"

"You don't think I should just pop round to his house and sort of beg and plead, do you?"

Monday August 9th
11:40 a.m.

I will never get over this, never.

Mum says there are plenty more fish in the sea. Why is she so obsessed with fish? At a time like this! She doesn't care about my feelings anyway.

No one does.

Wednesday August 11th
2:49 p.m.

Took Angus for a long, moody walk. Part of me really hates the Sex God. Sadly it's only a little tiny part of me (near my knee), the rest of me really, really likes him!!!!

3:00 p.m.

Even my breasts like him. They want to break out of my T-shirt and yell, "I love you, I love you!!!"

3:32 p.m.

I hope I am not being driven to the brink of madness by grief. They say that some people never get over things, like whatshername, Kathy Thing. The one who wandered over the moors at night yelling, "Heathcliff, Heathcliff, it's me a-Kathy come home again." Was that Kathy Brontë, one of the Brontë sisters? Or was that Kate Bush? Anyway, whoever it was wandered off into the rain and died from heartbreak. That will be me. I feel a bit tired now. If I just lie down here in the grass I might never be found.

3:35 p.m.
Angus keeps tugging at his lead. It was murder getting it on him but at least it means he can't savage any small dogs that we see.

4:00 p.m.
Famous last words. Angus saw a Pekinese and dragged me to my feet and halfway across a field before I managed to get him under control. He's senselessly brave. There is something about small dogs that really irritates him.

4:30 p.m.
Angus can fetch sticks!!! I was just carrying a stick along, hitting things with it. Then my arm got tired so I flung it away. And Angus pounced on it and dragged it back!! Superdooper cat!!!

5:00 p.m.

I wonder if I could get him to carry a little flask of tea round his neck in case I fancied a cuppa when we were having our walk?

Friday August 13th
My bedroom
1:00 a.m.

Hot and stuffy. Big full moon. Sitting on the windowsill. (Me, not the moon.)

1:05 a.m.

I hate him.

1:06 a.m.

Oh I love him, I love him.

1:10 a.m.

I hate him, but he will not break me. I will make him regret the day he said, "I know a bloke called Dave. He's a good laugh."

She who laughs last laughs last.

2:00 a.m.

I am going to be a heartless babe magnet as revenge.

2:05 a.m.

Oh no, no, that's not what I mean. I don't want to be a babe magnet, that would mean I was a lesbian.

2:05 and 30 secs

Still, what is wrong with that? Each to their own, I say. After all, Mum must have kissed Dad (erlack).

2:06 a.m.

If anyone asked me to comment on sexuality, say in the *Mail on Sunday* or something, I would say that it is a matter of personal choice and nothing to do with nosey parkers. Or else I would say, "Don't ask me, I am on the rack of love."

Sunday August 15th
In bed
9:40 p.m.

In bed early, healing my broken heart in the "privacy" of my bedroom.

9:41 p.m.

How can I stop Libby hiding her pooey knickers in my bed?

Monday August 16th
9:00 a.m.

Up. Up at nine a.m. in the holidays. Nine a.m.!! This just proves how upset I am.

Mum hasn't even noticed, of course.

"Mum, shouldn't even you be able to potty-train Libby by now? At this rate she'll be a pensioner and still pooing all over the place. She'll never get a boyfriend... Still, that will make two of us."

Tuesday August 17th
8:30 a.m.

I think I've lost a lot of weight from my bottom. No one has noticed. Mum just wanders around in a dream. She has got a calendar up in the kitchen with the days marked off until Vati gets back and a heart drawn round the date. How sad is that at her age? I said, "Don't worry yourself about my breakfast, Mutti. I'll get it myself, you get on with your own very important life."

She was humming and slathering herself with creams and ignoring me. So I said even louder, "Something quite interesting happened last night; I slit my throat and my head fell off. Have you seen it anywhere?"

Mum called from the bathroom. "Has Libby got her shoes on?"

"I think Mr Next Door might be another transvestite like Vati."

She came out of the bathroom then. "Georgia, is it possible for you to help at all? Where is your sister?"

"Mum, have you noticed anything unusual about me? I am not happy... in fact, I am very unhappy."

"Why? Have you broken a nail?" And she laughed in a very unpleasant way. Then she called out, "Libbsy, where are you, pet? What are you doing?"

I could hear Libby's muffled voice from Mum's bedroom and a bit of miaowing. Libby called, "Nuffing."

Mum rushed in there, saying, "Oh God."

I heard bang bang, and Mum yelling, "Libby, that is Mummy's best lipstick!"

"It looks nice!!!!"

"No, it doesn't... Cats don't wear lipstick."

"Yes."

"No, they don't."

"Yes."

"Owww, don't kick Mummy."

"Bad Mummy!!!"

Hahahaha. She who laughs last laughs... er... the last.

Thursday August 19th

11:00 a.m.

Raining. In August. Typical. Squelching along on my way to meet Mrs Big Knickers, I was thinking... I could either give in and be a miserable, useless person, like Elvis Attwood, our barmy, sad old school caretaker. Or if I truly gave up I could be like Wet Lindsay. When Robbie dumped her she got all pale and even wetter than normal. She was like an anoraksick. (A person who is both very thin and wears tragic anoraks.) I just made that up as a joke. Even though I am very upset I can still think of a joke. I'll tell Jas when I see her. As I was saying, before I so rudely interrupted myself, I could be a sad old sadsack or I could gird my loins and be like in that song. The one where you have to search for the hero within yourself.

Jas was waiting for me at the bus stop. She said, "Why are you walking in that stiff way?"

"I'm girding my loins."

"Well, it looks painful, like you've got a stick up your bottom. You haven't, have you?"

"You really are sensationally mad, Jas. In olden days people would have thrown oranges at you."

As I said, I can sometimes surprise myself with my own wisdomosity. And humourosity. Even in adversosity.

Monday August 23rd
2:10 a.m.
In bed. Oh God, it's so boring being broken-hearted. I've spent so much time in bed I'll probably start growing a long white beard soon, like Rip van Thing.

2:15 a.m.
Or perhaps I could just grow my eyebrows and train them into a beard.

2:48 a.m.
I can't sleep. I've gone all feverish now. I'm going to creep downstairs and get Mum's *Men are from Mars* book and do some more research.

3:35 a.m.

God, it's too weird. Apparently boys might seem like they like you to be all interested in them, but really they want you to be like a glacier iceberg sort of girl. So you have to play hard to get. That's where I must have gone wrong. I have been too keen, I must do glacial.

Thursday August 26th
10:33 p.m.

Same bat time. Same bat place. Same scuba-diving Barbie digging me in the back.

According to the next bit in Mum's book, boys are like elastic bands. Good Lord!

It doesn't mean that boys are made of elastic, which is a plus because nobody wants a boyfriend made out of rubber. On the other hand, if they were made out of rubber you could save yourself a lot of time and effort and heartache by just rustling one up out of a car tyre. But that is not what the book means. Boys are different from girls. Girls like to be cosy all the time but boys don't. First of all they like to get all close to you like a coiled-up rubber band, but after a while they get fed up with being too coiled and need to stretch

♡ 91

away to their full stretchiness. Then, after a bit of on-their-own stretchy, they ping back to be close to you.

Hmmm. So in conclusion on the boy front, you have to play hard to get (the glacier bit), and also let them be elastic bands. *Sacré bleu!* They don't want much, do they?

Friday August 27th
4:20 p.m.
Round at Jas's house. Been to town. I bought myself some new lippy to cheer myself up and Jas got a new hot air brush thing that gives you bouncability. She was making her hair all turn under at the ends.

As she was tonging away at her hair she said, "I looked for a bra but I can't get one small enough. In fact, I don't need one, I'm more like Kate Moss. You have to wear one though, don't you?... Because of the pencil-case test thing."

"Just pencil... the case was my mum."

"Yeah, but the pencil stuck, didn't it? You said that if it did you had to have help and support."

"I know what I said."

When Jas really annoys me (i.e. all of the time) I notice that her fringe is more fringey than normal, if you know what I mean.

Fringey went on, "I'm only saying – there's no need to have a nervy b."

Jas was really, really beginning to annoy me. A lot. All her things are really neatly put away which is the sign of a very dull person in my opinion. When Jas and I stalked Wet Lindsay and looked through her bedroom window all her things were very tidy as well. Jas even puts all her knickers in the same drawer.

Besides it being VERY dull to do that it would also be useless at my house as Libby mostly uses my knickers as hats for her dolls. Or Angus eats them.

To change the subject I said, In a really caring way, "When does Tom go off to work experience?"

Jas stopped hot brushing her hair then and looked all mournful. Hahahahaha. She said, "Next Saturday – it's going to be really horrible. Do you think he'll meet someone else in Birmingham?"

I looked wise and oracle-like and like I was really thinking (which I wasn't). I said, "Well, he's a young bloke and we all know what young blokes are like."

"Do we?"

I laughed bitterly.

She said, "Just because Robbie went off doesn't mean all boys do."

"It does... in Mum's book *Men are from Mars* it tells you all about it."

She was interested then and came and sat next to me. "What does it say in the book? Does it say Tom is going to go off with someone else?"

I said, "Yes it does, Jas. It says in the worldwide number one bestseller written by some bloke in America who has never met Tom, it says in Chapter Two, 'Tom Jennings definitely goes off with someone else when he goes to do work experience in Birmingham for a month.'"

She looked a bit miffed. "Well, what do you mean, then?"

I waited for a bit. Teach her to go on and on about my breasty problem and the fact that SG had left me.

"Can I try your new shiny lippy?"

She wasn't interested, it was all just me, me, me with her. She just went on about her problems.

"Anyway, Gee, what do you mean about this book? Isn't it American?"

"Yeah."

"Well it will be about American boys, then, won't it?"

"No, it's about boykind."

"Oh."

I paused. She looked all goggly and attentive, it was quite a nice feeling. Perhaps I might reconsider my career and think about becoming an Agony Aunt rather than a backing singer. Especially since I can't sing. But I know all about agony.

Jas was as agog as two gogs. She said, "Go on."

I explained, "Boys are like elastic bands."

"What?"

"Boys are like elastic bands."

"What?"

"Jas, if you keep saying 'what?' every time I say something we may be here for some centuries."

"Well, what do you mean 'like elastic bands'?"

"They like to be all close and then after a bit of being close they have to stretch and get far away... and you have to let them and then they spring back."

"What?"

"You're doing it again and it really annoys me. In fact, I will have to kill you now because I have a lot of untamed energy because of the Sex God. I'm going to have to give you a bit of a duffing up." And I shoved her.

She said, "Don't be silly and childish."

I said, "I'm not."

She got up and started making her hair have more bouncability with the air brush thing again. I waited until she had got it just right (in her opinion), then I hit her over the head with a pillow. She started to say, "Look, this is not funn–" but before she could finish I hit her over the head again with the pillow. And every time she tried to talk I did it again. She got all red-faced, which in Jas's case is very red indeed. It made me feel much better. Violence may be the answer to the world's problems. I may write to the Dalai Lama and suggest he tries my new approach.

My room
Midnight

I've got a plan. It involves the two "isities". They are "maturiosity" and "glaciosity". Firstly I have to prove to SG that I am very sophis and grown-up. Not a laughing hyena in a school uniform as he thought the last time he saw me. (This is the maturiosity bit.) Secondly I must be distant and alluring and play hard to get. (This is the glaciosity bit.)

The conclusion of these two parts is that SG comes springing back like an elastic band.

Saturday August 28th
2:10 p.m.

Phoned Jas.

I said, "I've worked out a plan."

She said, "I can't talk, Tom and I are going to choose my tattoo."

Huh. Typico.

Well, old huge knickers always puts her boyfriend first. Just as well I am so popular.

10:00 p.m.

In bed listening to a tape. Sadly it is "the Teddy Bears' Picnic". Libby has made me listen to it five times. If I try to turn it off she has a nervy spaz and growls at me.

I phoned up my "mates" earlier to go out, but they were all busy.

11:00 p.m.

I wonder if I had an emergency, like appendicitis or something, would my mates be too "busy" to come to the hospital?

11:30 p.m.

I have got a pain in my side. It might be a grumbling appendix.

11:32 p.m.

In blodge we learned that rabbits have got some sort of shrub growing in their appendix. How normal is that?

Sunday August 29th
6:30 p.m.

Mutti and Libbs have gone to visit the elderly mad. (Grandad.) Mum asked me if I would like to go, but I just looked at her with pity. Sadly she didn't get it and asked me again. I explained politely that I would rather put my head in a pair of Elvis Attwood's old trousers. She said I was a "horrid, bad-tempered spoiled brat". Fat chance I'm spoiled. I'm lucky if I get one square meal a week. I'm getting really, really thin. Apart from my nose. And basoomas.

8:00 p.m.

Ellen, Rosie and Jools came round and we sat on the wall, looking at boys. There are, it has to be said, a lot of fit-looking boys, but they haven't got that certain Sex God factor for me.

Mark (BG) went by with his girlfriend Ella. She is practically a midget. I thought he was taking a toddler for a walk. Rosie said, "So what happened with you and Robbie?"

I said, "he sent me a note and said that I should go out with some loser called Dave the Laugh."

Rosie said, "That's sort of dumping by proxy, isn't it?"

I said, "Are you supposed to be cheering me up?"

"But I thought you got to number six and everything."

"Yeah, but he said his parents would go ballisticisimus because I am so young. They'd think I was jail thing."

The Ace Crew were all full-on, attention-wise. Ellen even took her chewing gum out.

Jools said, "What is jail thing?"

I didn't really know actually but I improvised (lied). "Er... it's when you are underage and you go to... er... number eight with a boy."

Rosie said, "What, if you let a boy touch you above the waist you have to go to jail?"

I said patiently, "No, he has to go to jail."

Rosie said, "Well, that's it for Sven, then."

I said, "Fair enough." But I don't know what I am talking

about really. I'm all upset and confused and still have Herr Kamyer legs, even though it's the end of August.

Monday August 30th
1:43 p.m.

Borrowed Ellen's Kool Tan. Soon my Herr Kamyer legs will turn into sun-kissed boy magnets. Hmmm, smooth it on smoothy smooth and leave for an hour.

2:00 p.m.

If I move my bed and open the window I can sort of sunbathe on my bedroom floor. SG is going to find it damn difficult to resist the new tanned me.

4:05 p.m.

Woke up to orange Herr Kamyer legs and a huge red nose!!

5:00 p.m.

I've just scrubbed my legs off. They are not quite so orange but my nose looks like one of those red clown noses. Brilliant.

operation elastic band

Wednesday September 1st
7:00 p.m.

It's boiling having to wear stockings in this weather, but better than being blinded every time I look down at my still orangish legs.

Eight days till we go back to Stalag 14. I'm going to put my foot down with a firm hand this term and make sure I don't have to sit next to Nauseating P. Green.

Mum has gone out to Uncle Eddie's with Libbs. He is teaching Mum salsa dancing – can you imagine? How very sad. The tremendously old can be very embarrassing. Imagine my mum salsa dancing with Uncle Eddie the human boiled egg.

In public.

Or private.

7:05 p.m.

Jas called. Tom has gone off to work experience and she wants to come round. I am a substitute boyfriend. Well she can think again if she thinks I am going to be constantly available when Tom goes off to work experience. I am not so cheap.

7:08 p.m.

I may make her give me some expensive present that I choose from Boots. Oh no, hang on, I've got a better idea.

7:30 p.m.

Jas moaning on about Tom.

I listened sympathetically and said, "Shut up, now, Jas."

Then she looked at me. "Why have you got pink panstick on your nose?"

I said, "Shut up, now, Jas."

7:42 p.m.

I made my famous French toast for Jas. (Beat an egg and put bread in it and then fry it. The French bit comes in when you are eating the toast and you have to speak with a French accent.) As we were munching through the toast I said, "Jas, *ma petite.*"

"*Quoi?*"

"I've got *le plan* to *impressez* the Sex God *avec* my maturiosity. It involves *vous.*"

She almost choked on her toast. "*Non.*"

"You will *aime* it."

"Oh *mon Dieu.*"

The first part of my plan was that we got dressed up to look as old as we could and get on a bus and get full fares. As an experiment. She was grumbling as she got made up but at least she was on the move.

8:30 p.m.
Ready. I must say I think we looked v. Sophis. We'd got loads more make-up on than we normally wear, and darker lipstick. And we wore all black. Black is very ageing, as I continually tell Mum so I can get her black T-shirt and leather trousers. I said to Jas, "We'd better get back before she gets home because I have borrowed her Gucci handbag. She specifically said she would kill me if I ever borrowed it.

She is very, very mean with her things, which is why I have to borrow them in secret."

As we walked down the street I had another idea. "Let's keep pretending we are French as well."

"Why?"

"Don't you mean *pourquoi*?"

"No, I mean why?"

"Just *parce que, ma petite* pal."

Midnight

Oui!!! Très, très bon!! Merveilleux!!!! It was *très, très bon plus les grandes knobs.*

The bus driver was like a sort of mobile version of Elvis Attwood, our school caretaker – i.e. very old, mad and bad-tempered, but sitting in a bus rather than a hut. I said to Mobile Elvis, "*Bonsoir, mon très* old *garçon. Mon amie et moi désire deux billets pour* Deansgate, *s'il vous plaît.*"

He understood we wanted to go to Deansgate but unluckily, like all very old mad people, thought he could be funny and witty. He gave us the tickets (full fare! Yesss!!! Result!!!!). I handed over the money and he said, "*Merci*

buckets." Then he laughed himself senseless (easy enough as he was mad in the first place). I thought he would choke to death because he was laughing so much, but sadly he didn't.

What is the matter with people?

12:20 a.m.
Snug in my bed. Maybe I should leave school as I look so old.

2:30 a.m.
I could go off and have sophisticated adventures instead of hanging around with very young people.

12:35 a.m.
I could go to India and visit the Dalai Lama, or is it Gandhi who lives there? I don't know. We haven't done India in geoggers yet. All I know is what Mum tells me about it, and that is mostly, "Oh it was just so... you know... great." Anyway, even if we had done India in geoggers Mrs Franks is so bad at explaining things that I wouldn't know any more than I do now. She called concentration camps "contraception camps" while we were doing world affairs.

1:00 a.m.

Now on to part two of the plan. The glaciosity bit. I must look for an opportunity to show SG how stand-offish I can be.

Saturday September 4th

5:50 p.m.

Five days to Stalag 14 (school) and counting. I got my uniform out of the back of the wardrobe. Angus must have been using it as his lair by the look of it. I bunged it in the washing machine and hoped the bits of feather would come off.

I did cheer myself up a bit because I thought of something funny to do with my beret. Which we are forced to wear by the Oberführer (Miss "Hawkeye" Heaton).

6:00 p.m.

Phoned Rosie.

"I've thought of something really cool to do with the beret this term."

Rosie said, "I thought we were going to do the rolling it up into the sausage and pinning it under our hair at the back routine again?"

"Yeah I know, but what about this... what about if we use it as combination beret and lunchbox?"

Rosie said, "How do you mean?"

I had to explain, patiently. It is not easy being the leader of the gang. I sympathise with Richard Branson on this one, although I still see no reason for his ridiculous beard.

Anyway, I said, "Pop your sandwiches or crisps or whatever into the beret, then tie it on to your head with your scarf. *Voilà*, beret and lunchpack all in one."

"Hawkeye would go mad."

"Exactamondo, *ma petite amie.*'

Rosie said, "You are a genius." She is not wrong.

Sunday September 5th
5:10 p.m.

Au secours and *sacré bleu*!! Just walking to the park to meet the gang when I saw Call me Arnold, the vicar. I ducked down behind a car to hide until he had gone by. But the car was his car. When he got in he saw me crouching down. I had to pretend I was looking at a really interesting pebble.

God will know that I was hiding from his maidservant.

Still, I don't know how I could possibly be made to suffer more than I am already.

5:45 p.m.
Now I know. Cousin James is coming round tomorrow.

Midnight
If he gets all weird like he has done in the past and attempt to kiss me or anything, I may go mad.

Monday September 6th
10:00 p.m.
Cousin James asked me if I wanted to play strip poker. I was so embarrassed, I just said, "I don't know how to play poker," and he said, "Well, let's play strip snap, then."

I pretended I could hear the phone ringing. When he left, five million years later, I noticed there was something lurking under his nose. I thought it was a bogey at first, but sadly I now think it was a sort of moustache. Erlack!

Wednesday September 8th
10:00 p.m.

Mum came in my bedroom and asked if I wanted a wake-up call for Stalag 14 tomorrow. I said, "Oh, hello Mum, what are you doing in?"

She patted me on the head and said, "Goodnight, my sweet-natured little elf."

Nothing seems to bother her now that Vati is coming home. She might have put his moustache out of her mind but I haven't. In fact, to remind her I have drawn a moustache on the heart she put in the calendar.

10:30 p.m.

Washed my hair but couldn't be bothered drying it. I know if I sleep on it while it is damp I will wake up with the "stupid hedgehog" look. There will be bits sticking up all over the place, so I am sleeping with my pillow tucked under my neck and my head sort of drooping over the other side.

This is how Japanese Buddhist people sleep – it's probably whatsit... zen. They probably do it because it lets their chi flow free. Chi is energy that is in your body it says in my Buddhist book. Heaven knows I need as much energy as I can get for working out my plan for SG retrieval.

I think all the blood may have drained into my head from my shoulders.

11:00 p.m.

What happens if you get too much extra blood in your head? If you were meant to have two shoulders and a neck's worth of extra blood in your head you would have a bigger head, surely?

Or inflatable ears that could accommodate the extra blood and so on. Do Japanese have big ears?

Perhaps that is why Wet Lindsay's ears are so huge – because she's got Japanese ancestors. I wouldn't be surprised.

That would explain her tiny legs.

But not her big goggly eyes.

Thursday September 9th
8:00 a.m.

Woke up all snuggled down under the covers. I must have dropped asleep and forgotten about my zen position. My awake mind said, "Ha-so, I am a Japanese zen person ha-sleep with head h-over end of bed." But my English subconscious took over when I was asleep and said, "Snuggle down, you know you want to..."

Bathroom
8:10 a.m.
OhmyGodohmyGod... my hair looks like I've been electrocuted. No time to wash it. I'll have to gel it down.

8:30 a.m.
Pant pant, rush rush. Jas waiting for me.

She said, "Why do you look like Elvis Presley?"

As we ran up the hill towards school, we could see Hawkeye standing like a ferret by the gates. Oh here we go again... the beret patrol!!!! I hadn't got mine on. No time for the "sausage" or the "lunchpack". Only one thing for it. I fished the beret out of my bag and pulled it right down over my ears. You could only just see my eyes.

When we ran past Hawkeye she shook herself like something nasty had made a nest in her knickers.

"Two minutes to assembly; don't start the term with a detention."

♥ III

Oh very caring. "Hello, Georgia, welcome back," would have been nice.

As we dashed to the cloakroom I said to Jas, "Imagine her having a boyfriend! Erlack, no no, I must pull my mind away from that otherwise I'll start imagining her snogging or something. Urgh!!!! Urgh! I've done it now: I've let it in my brain!!! Hawkeye getting up to number seven on the snogging scale. Putting her tongue in someone's mouth. Maybe Herr Kamyer in his lederhosen. Urghhhh. Erlack. Get out, get out!!!"

I ripped off my beret and coat and went into the main hall.

Rosie, Ellen, Jools and Mabs – otherwise known as the Ace Crew – were all there. I gave them our special Klingon salute. They looked at me like they had never seen me before. Had they forgotten all we had shared after so little time? I felt a hand on my shoulder. It was Hawkeye. What fresh hell? She looked down her big beaky nose at me and hissed, "Take this, make yourself presentable and get back here as quickly as you can, you stupid girl."

I looked down and saw that she had given me a comb. When I went into the loos I saw my hair had gone the shape of my pulled-down beret because of the superdooper hair gel.

Sacré bleu! I feel like *un* nincompoop.

9:00 a.m.

Took my usual place next to Rosie and Jas. Our revered headmistress "Slim" Simpson (so called because she weighs about a ton) lumbered on to the stage. I whispered to Rosie, "Crikey, she has got chins on her chins."

Slim bored us half to death by telling us what fabulous treats were ahead of us this term. Exams (yippee!); the challenge of modern languages and physics with Herr Kamyer (superdooper!!!); a school trip to the escarpments of the Lake District (oh marvy!!!)...

As she said each thing Rosie and I were clapping our hands together in delight until Hawkeye gave us the evil eye. Good grief.

Break
11:00 a.m.

Jools, Ellen, Mabs, Rosie, Jas and I met behind the tennis courts for a confab. Elvis Attwood, the grumpiest caretaker in the universe, shouted at us as we passed his hut, "I've got my eye on you lot. Don't come sneaking into my hut otherwise there will be trouble."

He's beyond bonkerdom. He came to a school dance and did some exhibition twisting on stage until his back went and he had to be taken to casualty. That's when we started calling him Elvis.

I waved and shouted back, "Greetings, oh mad one."

We were grumbling and moaning as we sat down. As usual in this fascist hell-hole we have been split up in class and not allowed to sit together. I have my "pal" Nauseating P. Green next to me. She wears those glasses that look like they have been made out of jam jars, which is very unfortunate. She's got really bulgy eyes anyway. Rosie said, "I think there must be a touch of the goldfish in her family genes."

As we ate our snacks you could see right up Jas's skirt. I said, "Jas, do you always wear those huge knickers? A small dog could creep up a knicker leg and you wouldn't know."

"Well I like to be comfy."

"They're not very sexy, are they?"

"You said you thought little knickers were stupid. Remember Lindsay's thongs?"

"Shut up, don't upset me. You know how visual I am.

Now not only have I got Hawkeye snogging Herr Kamyer in my brain, I've also got Wet Lindsay's thongs."

Ellen said, "Anything happening with you and Robbie?"

I explained about my glaciosity and maturiosity plan. They all nodded wisely. We are a very wise group. Full of wisdomosity. I am almost certainly wiser than God, who doesn't seem able to grant the simplest of requests. Which is why I have turned to Lord Buddha.

Rosie spoilt the moment of wisdomosity by saying through a mouthful of cheesy snacks. "What in the name of pantyhose are you talking about?"

4:45 p.m.
At the end of my glorious day today Elvis made me pick up a sweet wrapper in the corridor. All because I did my VERY funny impression of him doing the twist and then his back going. If he doesn't want people to make jokes at his expense he should stay indoors. He's a barmy old fascist. I bet he goes round dropping sweet papers on purpose.

5:05 p.m.
Jas phoned, all breathless and excited.

"I've got two letters from Tom."

I said, "He's only gone to Birmingham."

"I know, but... well... you know."

No, I don't know.

5:15 p.m.

Libby and Mum came home. Libby has had her first day at kindergarten which I think is a good thing as it will make her less mad.

5:16 p.m.

Wrong. Libby has made me something to wear at kindergarten. She was ramming it on my head. I said, "Steady on, Libby, be gentle with my head. What is it you have made?"

"It's nice!!!"

"Yes. I know. But what is it?"

She looked at me like I was a halfwit and put her face nose to nose with mine. She said really slowly, "For... egg!!!"

"For my head?"

She hit me. "No, no, no, bad boy... for your EGG!"

Mum came in.

"Look, Georgie, she's made you an egg cosy."

"Well why is she trying to put it on my head?"

"She must have got mixed up. Maybe she thinks the teacher said 'head cosy'." And Mum started laughing like a drain. Libby joined in while I just sat there.

7:00 p.m.
What is there to laugh at? I am on the rack of love. Life is a sham and a facsimile and a farce.

7:15 p.m.
But at least I have an egg cosy.

8:00 p.m.
I am soothing myself by pampering my mind and body. I am pampering my mind by reading (an article about mascara) and I am pampering my body by eating a LOT of chocolate.

9:00 p.m.
Now I feel worried, fat, but very well informed about mascara. Which is a plus.

Wednesday September 15th
Assembly
9:00 a.m.

Does Slim go to a special evening class on how to be boring? She was going on about tiny people with small heads or the poor or something. I don't know, who cares? Well obviously someone cares, and maybe I will care again one day, but at the moment all my caringness is used up on myself.

RE
10:00 a.m.

Despite my tragedy I did cheer up a bit in RE. Honestly. Miss Wilson lives in the land of the very mad. Where does she get her stockings from? It can't be a normal shop. It must be a circus shop. They are all thick and wrinkly like an elephant has been wearing them. Perhaps they are Slim's cast-offs?

Rosie sent me a note: Dear Gee, Ask Miss Wilson if God has a penis.

Even in my tragedy it made me laugh and Miss Wilson said, "Georgia, what is funny? Perhaps you could share the joke with us all."

"Er... well, I was just wondering if God had..."

Rosie looked at me in amazement.

Miss Wilson was encouraging me in my religious curiosity. "You were wondering if God had...?"

"Yes, if God had a... beardy thing?"

Miss Wilson unfortunately did not realise how very funny I was being. She went on and on about the fact that he wasn't really a bloke with a beard in the sky but more of a spiritual entity. She didn't need to tell me that there is no big bloke in the sky. I know that. I've tried often enough to speak to him and get stuff. Hopeless. That is why if she had bothered to ask me I would have told her that I have become a zen Buddhist.

1:15 p.m.

What is it with Elvis? Jas and me were innocently moaning by the back of the science block and he comes along. Ears flapping in the wind. Raving on and on.

"What are you two up to?"

I said, "Nothing."

"Don't give me nothing. I know you two. You've probably been messing about in my hut."

What is the matter with him? And why does he always

wear a flat hat? I wonder if his head is flat underneath it? Probably. As we walked away I said to Jas, "He's obsessed with us going in his hut. He's ALWAYS saying we go in his hut. He goes on and on about it, like a budgie. Why does he go on and on about it?"

Jas was walking along. I said, "Why? On and on and on about us going in his poxy hut. Why us? Why keep accusing us of going in his hut? Why?"

Jas said, "Because we go in his hut."

"So?"

5:00 p.m.

Jas's room at her house. Jas has just popped down to the kitchen to make me some nutritious snack (Pop-Tarts) to cheer me up. I'm just not interested in anything, though.

5:03 p.m.

God her room is tidy. It's pathetically tidy. All her cuddly toys are neatly lined up in size order on her bed. I'm going to mix them up for a hilarious laugh. Ho hum, pig's bum. She's even got a box with "letters" written on it. I wonder if she's got a drawer that says "enormous pants" on it. There are some letters in the box. Probably private ones. It says PRIVATE on the top of them. Probably private, then. Probably letters that Tom has written to Jas. Very personal and private, I'd better put them away.

5:16 p.m.
She calls him HUNKY!!!! This is hilariously crap!! Absolutemento pathetico!!! HUNKY!!! Tom!!! Hahahahahaha.

5:18 p.m.
He calls her Po!!! Like in the Teletubbies. Good grief, that is sad.

5:19 p.m.
Po, for heaven's sake.

5:20 p.m.
My lips are sealed vis-à-vis Hunky and Po.

5:21 p.m.
Even though it is very very funny I must never mention Hunky or Po.

5:23 p.m.

Jas comes back in. I say, "How is Hunky?"

My bedroom
7:00 p.m.

Jas is not speaking to me because I happened to find some personal letters of hers... She's so touchy."

10:30 p.m.

And unreasonable.

Thursday September 16th
8:20 a.m.

On the way to school. When I got to our usual meeting place Jas had already set off, walking really fast ahead of me. I yelled, "Hang on a minute, Po!!" But she ignored me.

Honestly, people really take themselves seriously when they have got a so-called boyfriend.

In a sort of a way it was very funny walking behind Jas. She walked really fast for about five minutes but she is not in tiptop physical condition. In fact, the only exercise she gets is lifting Pop-Tarts and putting them in her mouth.

Anyway, she got tired and had to slow down so then I could catch her up. I walked about half a metre behind her: it was annoying her quite a lot but she couldn't say anything as she is not speaking to me.

By the time I got to the school gates I was walking about ten centimetres behind her. Her beret was practically sticking up my nose.

She tried to escape me in assembly by standing next to Rosie but I squeezed in between them and looked at her with my face really near hers. She was all red and furious. Even her ears were red. Tee hee.

11:00 a.m.
Followed Jas into the loos. I went into the next cubicle to her and talked to her through the walls.

"Jas, I love you."

"What are you doing? You're being stupid!"

"No. YOU'RE being stupid, Po."

"It was really mean of you to read my private letters."

"They were only from Hunky."

"You shouldn't read people's private things."

"How would I know anything if I didn't?"

123

There was a bit of a silence from the other side of the wall. Then she said, "What do you mean?"

I went on reasonably, "I wouldn't even know you were called Po if I hadn't read the letters."

She was on the edge of bamboozlement. "Yeah, but that's not the point... I..."

"You shouldn't have secrets from your very best pal."

"YOU have secrets."

"I don't – I even told you about my sticky-out nipples."

"Well, Tom says they stuck out because it was cold."

I couldn't believe it. The bell went for the end of break and I heard Jas flush the loo and go out. I rushed out of my loo and set off down the corridor, following her. "You told Tom... about my sticky-out nipples???"

I couldn't believe it. My nipples had been made a public mockery of a sham... I was so incensed I barely noticed Wet Lindsay talking to some unlucky fourth former. Although I did notice that she looked like an owl in a school uniform.

I was hissing at Jas. "You discussed my nipples with Hunky... I can't believe it!!!"

Then from behind me I heard Wet Lindsay's voice,

"Georgia, your skirt is tucked up in your knickers... I don't think it sets a very good example to the younger girls."

Then she went off, sniggering in a pathetic sniggering owl sort of way.

5:00 p.m.

In the bath. That is it. I am on the warpath. I am now a loner. I have no friends. My so-called best friend only likes stupid Hunky and discusses my private body parts with him. And then he probably goes and discusses it with his older brother. And he and the SG have a good laugh.

5:15 p.m.

Angus is sitting on the side of the bath. He is drinking the water even though it has got bubble bath in it. His whiskers are all soapy.

5:20 p.m.

Now Libby has wandered in. Come in, everybody, why don't you? I'm only having a bath. Naked. I'm surprised Mr and Mrs Next Door don't pop in for a bit of a look.

I said to Libby, "Libby don't push Angus like that, he'll—"

5:21 p.m.

Angus is soaking and furious. When I fished him out of the bath he savaged my hand. Libby couldn't stop laughing. What a life.

6:00 p.m.

Jas phoned. I said, "What do you want, nipple discusser?"

She said, "Look, can't we call it quits? I won't mention the Hunky business again if you forget about the nip nips incident."

I didn't want to give in because I was in too bad a mood so I just went, "Huh."

But then I was all agog attention-wise because she said, "Tom phoned and told me The Stiff Dylans are doing a gig at the Crazy Coconut club a week Wednesday. AND WHAT'S MORE Dave the Laugh is going to be there. AND WHAT'S MORE my mum is staying at my aunt's in Manchester."

6:02 p.m.
Thinking.

6:05 p.m.
Thinking and eating cornflakes. Hmmm.

6:07 p.m.

Obviously this is it!!! This is my chance to implement the elastic band theory. I have to go to The Stiff Dylans gig and get off with Dave the Laugh. In front of the SG. This will serve the twofold purpose of maturiosity (being at a nightclub) and glaciosity (getting off with another boy). SG will be very jealous. He will want to come pinging back (the elastic band theory).

11:00 p.m.

I must start softening Mum up so that she will not be suspicious when I say I am staying at Jas's on Wednesday night.

Saturday September 18th

Morning

10:00 a.m.

Mum nearly dropped Libby when I said, "Do you want me to get anything for you while I am in town this afternoon?"

She said, "Sorry, love, I thought for a moment you offered to do something for me. What did you really say?"

Even though I was irritated by her I kept a lovely smile on my face. "Oh Mutti... as if I never do anything for you!"

She said suspiciously, "Why are you smiling like that? What have you got on that is mine? If you have borrowed my gold necklace I'll go mad."

I snapped then. "Look, what is the matter with you? How can I ever be a nice person if you are so suspicious all the time? What are you, a mother or a police dog? Do you want to do a body search before I go out? Honestly!!!"

Then I remembered my Operation Elastic Band just in the knickers of time. I said nicely, "I just thought you might want me to bring something back for you. I know how busy you are, that's all."

In the end I think I convinced her, which is a bit of a drag as now I've got to lumber home with waterproof panties for Libbs. Hey ho. What sacrifices I make for the SG. I've almost forgotten what he looks like.

10:05 a.m.
I've remembered what he looks like. Yum yum yum.

1:00 p.m.

Miss Selfridge changing room. I tried on a size twelve T-shirt and I couldn't get it on. Jas (very loudly) said, "I think your breasts are definitely getting bigger, you know."

This was in the packed communal changing room and everyone looked round.

I said, "Er... Jas... I think there is someone in Australia who might not have heard you properly."

Rosie and Ellen met us in Luigi's coffee bar. I told them about The Stiff Dylans gig and my plan vis-à-vis Dave the Laugh. Rosie was eating the foam from her coffee with a spoon and slurping. So was Ellen. It was stereo foam slurping. After ten years had gone by Rosie said, with the spoon in her mouth which was very unattractive but I didn't say... anyway, she said, "So you're going to the gig so that you can get off with Dave the Laugh and that will make the SG into an elastic band?"

How difficult can life be? Very, very difficult, that's how. I said patiently (well, at least without hitting her), "Yes, yes, thrice yes!!!"

More slurping. She was obviously thinking about my masterplan (or mistressplan actually, as I had thought of it and I am a girlie). Then she said, "Can I borrow your brown leather boots?"

4:00 p.m.

Lugged home Libby's waterproof nick-nacks. All quiet on the home front when I got in. Where was everyone?

9:30 p.m.

Early to bed, early to rise, makes a... whatsit.

10:00 p.m.

I may wear some false eyelashes for the gig. I must be careful though, last time I tried them the glue tube burst and I couldn't get my eyes apart for twenty minutes.

Tuesday September 21st
4:15 p.m.

Boring day apart from when Wet Lindsay got her bag caught on her foot and fell up the science-block stairs.

11:00 p.m.

Libby in bed with me. I don't know why she can't sleep the right way up, her feet keep poking me in the eye.

11:10 p.m.

I wonder what Dave the Laugh looks like?

Friday September 24th
Morning break
11:00 a.m.

Ellen told me that her brother and his mates go out on "cat patrol".

I said, "Do they really like cats, then?"

She said, "No, him and his mates are the cat patrol and they go out looking for birds... you know, chicks... girls."

Good Lord.

Lunchtime
12:30 p.m.

Ellen says that her brother also calls breasts "nunga-nungas".

I know I shouldn't have asked but somehow I just had to.

Ellen said, "Well, he says that if you get hold of a breast and pull it out and then let it go... it goes nunga-nunga-nunga!"

I may be forced to become either a celibate or a lesbian.

Afternoon break
2:30 p.m.

Me and Ellen were sitting in the loos with our feet up against the back of the doors, so that the Hitler Youth (prefects) wouldn't know we were in there and send us into the torrential rain. The Hitler Youth call it a "slight shower". They'd still say that if the First Years were being swept to their deaths by tidal waves. Or if Elvis's hut was bobbing along with a sail up, or... anyway, who cares what they say?

I said to Ellen through the cubicle wall, "Is your brother a bit on the mad side?"

I could hear her crunching her crisps. She thought about it. "No, he's quite a laugh, really. He calls going to the loo 'going to the piddly-diddly department'."

I could hear her through the wall, laughing and choking. I just sat there staring at the loo door. After a bit she controlled herself and said, "If he's going to the loo to do number twos he says, 'I'm just off to the poo-parlour division'." And she was off, wheezing and choking again. *Sacré bleu.* I am surrounded by *les idiots.*

3:30 p.m.

If it's cold, Ellen's hilarious brother says it is "nippy noodles".

4:15 p.m.

Walked home. Thinking about the difference between girls and boys. For instance, when girls walk home we put on lippy and make-up. We chat. Sometimes we pretend to be hunchbacks. But that is it. Perfectly normal behaviour. When the Foxwood boys come out they hit each other, trip one another up and stuff leaves or caps down each other's trousers. Ellen told me that sometimes her brother sets fire to his farts.

On the way to my house we passed through the park. There is a park Elvis. He is supposed to be the park keeper but mainly he prods at things with a pointy stick. Oh and his second job is to yell, "I can see you!" at innocent snoggers in bushes.

We hung around on the swings for a bit just to annoy Park Elvis. Rosie (who by the way, since the flaming fringe incident is an ex-smoker) said she had made it up with Sven her Swedish boyfriend. She fell out with him because he said to her parents, "Thank you for your daughter, she is, how you say? *Jah...* a great SNOG."

I said, "How can you tell he's sorry? No one can usually understand a word he says."

And she said, "He knitted me a nose warmer."

It's really not worth asking.

Ellen said, "What about Dave the Laugh?"

I said, "What about him?"

"Well, do you really fancy him?"

"I don't know. I don't know what he looks like."

"Well, what is the point, then?"

"Well, he's like... erm... a red herring. In my elastic band strategy."

They all looked at me. It was no use them all looking at me like I know what I am talking about. I'll be the last one to know what I am talking about, believe me.

4:30 p.m.

My so-called private bedroom.

Angus was in my bed. I suspect not alone. I daren't lift the cover in case it's like in that film where there was a chopped-off horse's head in the bed.

6:07 p.m.

Lying on the floor on cushion but at least Angus is nice and comfy. In Mum's *Cosmo* it says, "Buddhism is the new optimism."

Okey-doky. That's what I'm going to do. Be a cheery Buddhist. Om hahaha om.

Monday September 27th
Sports
2:50 p.m.

It's windy and rainy. Naturally these two facts mean that Miss Stamp our games mistress (who is definitely Hitler reincarnated in a gym skirt... she even has the little black moustache)... Anyway, these two facts mean that Adolfa has decided that the best thing we can do is... play hockey outside!!! I'd write to the newspapers to complain but I'll probably drown out on the hockey pitch.

In bed
9:30 p.m.

Brrr. If I have pneumonia and die and never get to number ten on the snogging scale I'll blame Adolfa. Just because she doesn't have a life. Even now I'm only just getting feeling back in my bottom.

10:30 p.m.

When Mum said goodnight I took my opportunity and said, casually, "Mum, can I go and stay round at Jas's on Wednesday night? Her mum says it's OK if it's OK with you. We're doing a science project together... I mean me and Jas not me and Jas's mother – that would be stupid."

(Shut up, shut up now. Leave it! Don't babble on, she'll get suspicious and you will say something really stupid.)

Mum said, "You don't usually do your homework, Gee. This is a bit of a change of heart."

"Hahahaha – yeah right... I..." (Careful, careful, don't say anything stupid.) "...I... thought I might be a scientist." (Too late, she's bound to rumble me now!)

"A scientist – not a backing singer, then?"

"No."

"Hmmm."

"So can I?"

"Oh yes, I suppose so. Night-night."

Result!!!!!! Yesssss!!!!

Wednesday September 29th
Operation Elastic Band
Kitchen
8:00 a.m.

I grabbed a piece of toast and mumbled, "I'm off now, see you tomorrow night."

Mum didn't even look up from trying to fasten Libby into her dungarees. Libby had her porridge bowl on her head. Mum said, "OK, love, bye. Kiss your sister bye-bye."

I said, "Pass," I had kissed Libby before when she had been eating porridge and I didn't want the experience again. I blew her a kiss. "Byeeeeee!"

Phew. Now then, quickly out of the door. Victory!!!!! I've packed all my clubwear and make-up and so on in my rucky. Here we go with Operation Elastic Band.

Just at the end of the path when Mum came out of the house, shouting, "Georgie, what do you mean, 'See you tomorrow night'?"

OhmyGodohmyGodohmyGod.

I laughed casually (sounding a bit like a casual hyena). "Oh I knew you would forget, I'm staying at Jas's tonight – remember?"

She looked blank.

Inwardly I was shouting, "LET ME GO!! SHUT UP, SHUT UP!! I MUST HAVE THE SEX GOD. LET ME GO. LET ME GO. YOU HAVE HAD YOUR LIFE!!!!" Outwardly I said, "Mum, I have to go, I'll be late – see you tomorrow."

Yessss!!! I am cool as *le* cucumber. Or possibly *le* ice cube.

3:50 p.m.

Last bell. Jas and I ran down the hill. Only five hours to get ready.

I said to Jas as we ran, "Mutti was really suspicious this morning when I reminded her I was staying at your house. It was like she didn't believe me. You know, like I am bound to be lying."

"You are lying."

"Oh picky, picky, Jas."

Jas's house
5:00 p.m.

A nourishing meal to set us up for the evening: oven chips, mayonnaise and two fruit Pop-Tarts (for essential vitamin C). In Jas's room we put on some groovy music and started

138

getting ready. Jas had a bit of a moony attack when she looked at Tom's photo by her bed. She started sighing and saying, "I just can't seem to get in the mood to go out."

I pointed at her with my mascara brush. "Jas, snap out of it, you know that Hunky would want you to go out. He phoned you up to tell you about it. He wouldn't want you moping about: he wouldn't want you to let your mates down by staying in. He wouldn't want to come home and find out that your mate had stabbed you with a mascara brush."

Jas was a bit huffy, but she got my nub. As she was putting her hair up she said, "What will you do with Dave the Laugh when you have got off with him?"

"How do you mean?"

I was stalling for time. I'd only really thought as far as getting my make-up on. The rest of it was a bit of a haze of a dream.

"Well, will you be... like his girlfriend then? Will you snog him?"

Luckily the phone rang. We both answered it. It was Rosie. She and Sven were calling from a phone box.

"We just rang to say we've made up this great new dance; it's called 'the phone box'."

She played a radio down the phone and in the background I could hear a lot of grunting and shuffling and Sven going, "Oh *jah*, Oh *jah*, hit it, lads!" or something in Swedish or whatever it is he speaks. Gibberish, normally. Not English, anyway. Then there was a bit of what sounded like tap-dancing. Rosie came back on the phone all breathless. "Brilliant, eh? See you in the next world... don't be late!" And she slammed the phone down.

9:15 p.m.
Left the house to catch the bus down town to the Crazy Coconut. I had so much make-up on I could hardly move my face, which is a plus really because it meant I wouldn't be tempted to go for full-on smiling. I was a vision in black leather. Prayed to God Mutti didn't go through her wardrobe before I could sneak things back in.

When the bus arrived and we got on I couldn't believe it. The driver was Mobile Elvis!! Sadly he remembered us and said "*Bonsoir*". And charged us full fare.

Crazy Coconut
9:30 p.m.

Rosie and Sven turned up. Sven was wearing silver flares. Good Lord. When he saw us he started twisting his hips, saying, "*Jah*, groovy. Let's go, babies!!!!"

The whole queue was looking.

I said to Rosie, "Does Sven always have to be so Svenish?"

Then the van with The Stiff Dylans in it arrived. Robbie got out. Oh bum, all my glaciosity turned to jelliosity.

He saw us and said, "Hi."

I went, "Nung." (I don't know what "nung" means, it just came out.)

The queue started to move and he sort of looked at me for what seemed ages, then he said, "Don't get into any trouble."

I was so mad. How dare he tell me not to get into any trouble? Now he had said that I was going to get into LOADS of trouble just to show him.

I'd show him how much maturiosity I had. At least I would if I managed to get in past the bouncers without them saying I was under age. I said quietly to Rosie and Jas and Sven, "Be really cool."

That's when Sven lifted me up under one of his huge Swedish type arms and shouted at the bouncers, "*Gut* evening, I have the bird in the hand and one in the bushes, thank you!" and strode in.

I don't know whether they let us in because we looked mature or whether they were so amazed by Sven they didn't notice us.

Anyway, Operation Elastic Band was underway.

11:00 p.m.

Us girls went to the loos and did some emergency make-up repair work. It was quite dark and sort of red lightish in the loos. I was just thinking we looked like groovy chicks around town when the Bummer Twins walked in. I say walked but they waddled. Jackie was wearing a dress that was SO tight. Not a wise choice for a girl who is not small in the bottom department. She is so common. They were both smoking fags (*quelle surprise*). Jackie said, "Oh look, they must be having a sort of crèche here while the grown-ups are clubbing."

She went off into the loo. I could hear her weeing. It sounded like a carthorse. Alison was looking down her nose at us. I'm surprised she could see anything past the huge spot that was on it. She looked like she'd got two noses.

The club was amazing. It had loads of flights of stairs all leading down to a big dance floor, and a stage at one end. You had to go down the stairs from the loos to get to the dance floor. I hoped that no one could see up my skirt because I couldn't remember what knickers I had on. Jas would be all right with her biggest knickers known to humanity.

There were flashing lights and mirror balls and laser beams. The music was really loud and rocking. Rosie and Sven did their phone box dance. Sven was yelling "Whoop!" and "Hit it, lads!" They had loads of space to dance in because nobody wants to be flattened by a huge bloke in silver trousers.

Jas shouted in my earlug. "There's a gang of Tom's mates by the bar – can you see them? Over there. Dave the Laugh is probably one of them."

Jools said, "Yeah, but which one? There's ten of them to choose from."

I said, "Is anyone laughing?"

Jools looked at me. "Why?"

"Well, if he's called Dave the Laugh everyone will be laughing around him."

We looked across at the lads who were mostly looking around the room. Then I had another thought. "But what if he is called Dave the Laugh because HE laughs all the time?"

We looked again; now they were all laughing.

Jas for once in her life went all decisive and sensible (it was a bit scary, actually). She said, "I recognise one of them, he's called Rollo, he's been round to Tom's house. I could ask him who Dave the Laugh is."

I said, "Yeah, OK, but be really cool, Jas. Just find out which one is Dave the Laugh so we can look at him. But don't mention anything about anything."

Jas said, "I am not a fool, you know."

I didn't know that, actually.

Jas went over to the lads and I could see her going chat, chat, nod, nod, nod, wiggle, wiggle, wiggle, flickey fringe, flickey fringe... (Why does she do that? It is so annoying.)

I was acting really cool, doing a half-smile and sort of nodding along to the music. Sipping my drink, waving at people, even ones I didn't know. Then Jas came back. She was all breathless. She POINTED really obviously at a dark-haired boy in black combats. "That's him!"

Naturally he saw her pointing at him and he shrugged his

144

shoulders like he was asking a question. Jas then turned to me and POINTED again... AT ME, and nodded like one of those nodding dogs.

I couldn't believe it. It was unbelievable, that's why. My face was like a frozen fish finger. All rigid and pale. (But obviously not with breadcrumbs on it.)

I said out of the corner of my mouth, "Jas, I'm going to kill you. What in the name of your huge knickers have you said?"

Jas said huffily, "I just said, 'Who is Dave the Laugh?' and Rollo said, 'This is Dave the Laugh,' and Dave the Laugh said, 'Why?' and I just said, 'Because my mate Georgia really rates you'."

I was going to kill her and then eat her.

Out of the corner of my mouth – because Dave the Laugh was still looking – I said, "Jas! You told him I FANCIED him? I cannot believe it."

Jas said, "Well I think he's quite cute. If I didn't have Hunky I would..."

Just then SG walked by carrying his guitar. On his way to the stage to do the first set. He smiled as he passed. Even though in my heart I wanted to leap into his arms like a seal I ignored him. I looked through him as if he was just a floating guitar in midair.

Midnight

The Stiff Dylans were playing and I was dancing with Rosie and Sven and Jas. Jools and Ellen had gone off with some of Tom's mates. They were all quite fit-looking boys, actually, but... there is only one Sex God on the planet. SG looked sooooo cool; it's not fair that he is so good-looking. All the girls were looking at him and dancing in front of him. They had no style. Every time he came off stage there would be some girl talking to him. I tried not to look but I couldn't help it. What if he got off with someone in front of me? How could I bear it? There was a moment when our eyes met and he smiled. Ooohh, Blimey O'Reilly's trousers, he'd got everything... back, front, hair, teeth... I could feel my snogging muscles all puckering up but I thought NO! Think Elastic Band.

I made Jas go to the loos with me for a bit of a break from the tension. The Bummer Twins were still in there. I could hear them talking from one of the cubicles and a spiral of smoke coming under the loo door. Do they live in the lavatories? I said to Jas, "Perhaps the Bummer Twins have trouble in the poo-parlour department!!" and we both got the hysterical heebie-jeebies. I had to hit Jas on the back to

146

stop her choking to death. And we had to reapply mascara twice.

On our way back to the dance floor Dave the laugh stopped me!! He said, "Hi."

I said, "Oh hi." (Brilliant.) And I half-smiled, remembering to keep my nose sucked in.

He said, "Are you Georgia?"

1:00 a.m.
Dave the Laugh is actually nice-looking in a sub SG way... and er... quite a good laugh.

2:00 a.m.
Dave the Laugh has been dancing with me a lot. He's a cool dancer. He even did a bit of mad dancing with Sven. I don't think he expected Sven to pick him up and kiss him on both cheeks, but he took it well. We all left the club together. I saw SG looking over at us as he cleared up his gear. There was some drippy blonde hanging about wanting his autograph or something (on yeah! Emphasis on the something). Time for a display of maturiosity and glaciosity. Dave the L. said, "Georgia, are you walking to the night bus stop?"

I made sure that SG was looking then I laughed like a loon on loon tablets. "Hahahahaha, the night bus! You make me die, Dave, you're such a laugh!!!!"

Dave looked a bit on the amazed side. He probably didn't think the night bus was his biggest joke. Me and Jas and Dave walked along. When we got to the bus stop there was a bit of an awkward pause. Jas was standing really close by like a goosegog. How was my plan vis-à-vis getting Dave the L. to go out with me going to happen if she just hung about like a goosegog? I kept raising my eyebrows at her but she said, "Have you got something in your eye? Let's have a look."

As Mrs Big but Stupid Knickers was prodding about at my eye Dave's bus came. He gave me a peck on the cheek and said, "Well, this is my bus. It was a great night; maybe see you later." He looked me in the eyes for a second, winked and then got on the bus.

As Mrs Loonyknickers Goosegoghead (Jas) and I walked home I was all confused.

"Does Dave the Laugh like me or not? He winked at me – what does that mean? SG definitely noticed us leaving, didn't he? And he saw me really laughing at what Dave the Laugh was saying."

Jas said, "That's when I thought Dave the Laugh might have gone off you, because he said, 'Are you catching the night bus?' and you nearly split your tights in half laughing. Your face went all weird and your nose sort of spread all over your—"

"Jas."

"What?"

"Shut up."

"Well, I was just saying."

"Well don't."

"Well I won't, then."

"Well don't."

"I won't."

"Well don't."

There was a bit of welcome silence for a bit then Jas said, "I won't."

She is so INCREDIBLY annoying.

3:00 a.m.

And she takes up loads of room in bed. I had to make a sort of barrier out of her cuddly toys to put down the middle of the bed. To keep her on her own side.

What does Dave the Laugh mean, "See you later"?

3:30 a.m.

Do I want to see him later even if he does mean "See you later"?

4:00 a.m.

If the Sex God was really jealous he would ring me up tomorrow and try to get me back.

Or maybe he is not fully extended elastic band-wise.

Thursday September 30th
3:00 p.m.

I fell asleep in German. Herr Kamyer is a very soothing teacher. I drifted off when he started telling some story about Gretchen and a dove in a dovecote. (Don't even ask, as I have mentioned before, the Germans are a mystery to me since I learned about the Heimlich manoeuvre.)

4:30 p.m.

On the way home we practised our new grasp of the German language.

I said to Jas, "What is 'a dove in a dovecote' in the German type language?"

Jas said, "Er... '*ein Duff in ein Duffcot*', I think."

150

"*Ach gut... so... Jas... Du bist ein Duff in Duffcot nicht wahr?*"

Jas said, "*Nein, ich nicht ein Duff in Duffcot.*"

I said, "*Jah.*"

Jas said, "*You have just said I am a dove in a dovecote.*"

"You are."

"You're bonkers."

I think I might be hysterical.

4:45 p.m.

So tired when I got in that I thought I would just have a little snooze.

5:00 p.m.

"Ginger, ginger, me home!!!"

Oh Lord, it was my dearly beloved sister. I heard her clattering up the stairs. Then a bit of deep breathing, and bumping, "Here we are, Ginger."

Then she and Angus got in bed with me. And they weren't alone. There was scuba-diving Barbie and Charlie Horse. And something really cold and slimy.

I shot up in bed and looked down at her. "Libbs, what is that?"

She gave me her idea of a lovely smile, which in her case

♥

is terrifying. She scrunches up her nose and sticks her teeth out. I don't know why she thinks that is natural. She said, "It's nice."

I looked under the covers. "What is? Oh God."

Mum called up, "Libbs, where has your jelly rabbit gone?"

Giganticus pantibus

Monday October 4th
9:30 a.m.
No news from either SG or Dave the so-called Laugh.

Geoggers
10:00 a.m.
Brrr. It's only October and it's like Greenland here. Well, apart from the ice floes and Eskimos and polar bears. It is, as Ellen's amusing brother would say, very "nippy noodles" today. I didn't mean ever to start saying things like that, but it is really catching. What's more, just because I said it all the gang is saying it. It's like brain measles. In geoggers Rosie put up her hand and said to Mrs Franks (who is not what you would call "fun"), "Mrs Franks, could I just pop to the piddly-diddly department, please?"

Mrs Franks said, really frostily, "What is the piddly-diddly department, Rosemary?"

And Rosie said, "Well it's not the poo-parlour division."

We all laughed like stuffed animals. Mrs Franks didn't. In fact she said, "Grow up, Rosemary Barnes."

She let Rosie go though, and started to explain something indescribably boring about the wheat belt. Behind her Rosie started lolloping out of the door like an orang-utan. She was trailing her arms on the floor. It made me laugh A LOT. But silently, as no one really wants to do two hours' detention.

Break
11:00 a.m.

They are a bunch of sadists here. We get forced to go out into sub-Antarctic conditions. Even Elvis Attwood won't come out of his hut and he is half human, half walrus. Meanwhile the so-called prefects and staff get to hang around in the warm. Wet Lindsay, the Owlie One, said to me, "If you wore skirts that were a bit longer you might not be so chilly."

I said to Jas, "Did you hear a sort of hooting noise, Jas?"

Me and Jas sheltered out of the icy winds behind a wall but we were still cold, so we had an idea. We thought we would button our two coats together to make a kind of big sleeping bag. We fastened the buttons of Jas's coat into the buttonholes of mine. Then we buttoned the buttons of my coat into Jas's buttonholes. With us in the middle. All nice and snug. It did make it very difficult to walk and unfortunately we had buttoned ourselves up a bit far away from our bags. Our bags with our nutritious snacks in them (Mars Bars and cheesy snacks). We tried synchronised shuffling to get to them but Jas tripped and we fell over. We were laughing, but not for long, because the Bummer Twins arrived.

Jackie looked down at us all tied together in our coats and said, "Look, Ali, the little girls are playing a little game. Let's join in."

And then they sat on us.

And they are not small girls.

Alison said, "Fancy a fag, Jackie?"

We heard them light up. We were just trapped there.

Then Jackie said, "Oooh look, someone has left some cheesy snacks for us. Fancy one, Ali?"

Me and Jas were the Bummer Twins' armchair.

My bedroom
5:30 p.m.
No phonecalls.

Mutti came in.

I said, "Oh come in, Mum, the door is only closed for privacy." I said it in a meaningful way but she didn't know what I meant. She was all pink.

"Dad phoned again; he sends his love, he's really looking forward to seeing you. He's got you a present."

I said, "Oh goodie, what is it? Sheepskin shorts?"

She started that tutting thing.

I don't think she has asked me one thing about myself for about four centuries. What is the point of procrastinating... no I don't mean that, what do I mean? Oh yeah... procreating... What is the point of having children if you are not going to take any notice of them? You might as well get a hamster and ignore that.

5:35 p.m.
Oh yippee.

This is my gorgeous life:
1. I haven't been kissed for a month; my snogging skills will be gone soon.

2. I have a HUGE nose that means I have to live for ever in the Ugly Home. Address:

Georgia Nicolson

Ugly Home,

Ugly Kingdom,

Ugly Universe.

3. My Red Herring plan has failed.

4. I am the Bummer Twins' armchair.

6:00 p.m.

Mum called up. "I'm just taking Libbs to the doctors'; she needs her ears cleaning out."

Oh please. Save me from that thought.

6:30 p.m.

Phone rang. If it's Po moaning on about Hunky I'll go BERSERK!!

6:45 p.m.

I'm seeing Dave in the swing park after school on Friday. He got my phone number from Tom through Jas! Good grief. The Red Herring has landed. I'm quite excited, I think.

Am I?

He said it would be "groovy" to see me again.

He also said he hoped it wouldn't be too nippy noodles in the park. He made me laugh.

I am still only using him as a red herring, though.

8:00 p.m.

Mum came back with Libby. I was busily trying to save myself from starving to death by eating cornflakes.

I said, "The doctor didn't find my fishnet tights in Libby's lugholes, did he?"

Mum seemed to be in even more of a coma than normal. She said, "I borrowed them for salsa dancing with Uncle Eddie."

Charming. I'll have to boil them before I wear them again.

Mum said, "They've got a new doctor at the surgery."

Silence.

"He's very good."

Silence.

"He was so nice to Libby – even when she shouted down his stethoscope."

What is she going on about?

"He looked a bit like George Clooney."

158

9:40 p.m.

When I went up to bed she kissed me and said, "You haven't had your tetanus injection renewed, have you?"

What is she talking about?

Tuesday October 5th

10:30 a.m.

Rosie said she might go across to Sweden land with Sven in the Chrimbo hols. I said, "Are you sure? You're only fourteen and you've got your whole life ahead of you. Are you sure you want to go to the other side of the world with Sven?"

She said, "What?"

I said, "Going to the other side of the world with Sven – is it a good idea?"

She said, "You don't know where Sweden is, do you?"

"Don't be stupid."

And she said, "Where is it, then?"

I looked at her. Honestly. As if I don't know where Sweden is. I said, "It's up at the top."

"Top of what?"

"The map."

And she went, "Hahahahahahahaha."

I think she must be a bit hysterical.

I may forgive her. Because so am I.

Maths
10:35 a.m.

Oh good grief, welcome back to the land of the crap. The Bummer Twins sent round a note: *Meet in the Fourth Year classroom as 12.30 today. Everyone comes, and that means you, Georgia Nicolson and your lesbian mates.*

I wrote a note to Jas and the others.

Dear Fab Gang,

This is it. Things have got sheer desperadoes. We have to put our feet down with firm hands. I for one am no longer prepared to be the Bummer Twins' armchair!!! Meet in the science block at 12.15. Or be square.

Gee-gee

xxxxxxx

12:32 p.m.

Hiding from the Bummer Twins in the science-block loos. Jas, Jules, Rosie, Ellen, Patty, Sarah, Mabs and me... all in one cubicle. We have to keep our feet off the floor so that no one will know we are in here. It's hard to keep your balance when there are eight of you standing on one loo seat.

Alert, alert!!!! Two people came into the loos. I recognised their voices. It was Wet Lindsay and one of her mates, Dismal Sandra.

Wet Lindsay said, "Honestly, some of the younger girls are so dim. One of them came to see me and asked me if she could get pregnant from sitting on a boy's knee."

Jas mouthed at me, "Can you?" Which I thought was quite funny but I couldn't laugh otherwise we would end up quite literally down the pan.

I wanted to look over the top of the cubicle so that Owlie would know I had seen her in the loo. Seen her removing her thong from her bum-oley!!!

Then Owlie's weedy mate Dismal Sandra said, "What's happening with Robbie?"

I was full-on, attention-wise.

Wet Lindsay said, "Well he says he doesn't want to get serious because of college and the band and everything."

I nearly yelled out, "It's not that, Owlie, it is because he DOESN'T like you..."

Dismal Sandra said, "So what will you do, then?"

Lindsay said, "Oh, I've got my ways, I'll charm him back in the end. He's not seeing anyone else, he says. I expect he's still upset about us splitting up."

Oh yeah, in your dreams, Owlie.

Physics
1:30 p.m.

Herr Kamyer was twitching about in his sad suit. It's sort of tight round the neck and short round the ankles. Do normal people wear tartan socks? Anyway, he was adjusting his spectacles and saying, "So zen, girls, ve haf the interesting question about ze physical world. Ver question is (twitch twitch), vich comes first... ze chicken or ze eggs?"

No one knows what he is talking about so we just carried on writing notes to each other or making shopping lists. Ellen was actually painting her toenails. You would think that Herr Kamyer would notice that she had her head underneath the desk, but he didn't seem to.

He really does jerk around. He sort of blinks his eyes and screws up his nose and flings his head round all at once. Someone said it was because he has had malaria. Once when he was walking across the playground and it was icy he had such a spasm that he slipped and crashed into the bike shed. Elvis had to restack sixty bikes. He grumbled for about forty years. You would think Elvis would have more sympathy for the afflicted. As he is so afflicted himself.

Suddenly about ten girls started sneezing really violently. Really violently, like their heads were going to blow off. Their eyes were streaming and they were stumbling for the door. Jackie Bummer managed to say, "Oh we must be... ATISHOO... ATISHOO... allergic to something in the science lab, Herr Kamyer. ATISHOO!"

They all got sent home in the end.

I found out later what the Bummer Twins' meeting was about. They had made everyone at the meeting put bath crystals up their noses in the middle of physics, and that had brought on the sneezing attacks. All because the Bummers wanted to go to some club in Manchester, and needed to be home early.

Good Lord. Three days to my date with the Herring.

5:00 p.m.

Jas made me go home with her. She is planning a special celebration for when Tom gets home.

"It will be one year since we first met on the day he gets back!"

I just looked at her.

"And look!" Before I could stop her, she pulled up her skirt and pulled down her voluminous pants to show me her stupid heart tattoo. "I've been washing round it!"

She went on and on about what she was planning to do. Even though I found some matchsticks and put them over my eyelids so it looked like they were holding my eyes open. Eventually I said, "Look, why don't you do a nice vegetable display for him?"

Midnight

Honestly, Jas is so mad and touchy. And violent.

Wednesday October 6th
4:30 p.m.

After swimming today Miss Stamp came into the showers to make sure we all went in. She says we pretend to have a shower and that we are unhygienic. That is why she must supervise us. But really it is because she is a lesbian.

She watched a few of us go through (twirling her moustache). She shouted, "Come on, you silly ninnies, get in and get out!"

I dashed in in the nuddy-pants and was soaping myself like a maniac in order to get out quickly because Miss Stamp is a lesbian and might... well might... er... look at me. As if that wasn't bad enough I had to be on even more red alert because Nauseating P. Green lumbered into the shower next to me. What if she accidentally touched me? It's a sodding nightmare this place, like the Village of the Damned. If P. Green fell against me I would be smickled with Nauseatingness. She really is a most unfortunate shape. What on earth does she eat? All the pies, that is for sure. In fact, she has no shape. You can only tell which way up she is because of her glasses.

As I was getting dried I did feel a bit sorry for her because the Bummers had hidden her glasses while she was in the shower. She blundered around in the elephantine nuddy-pants, looking for them. The Bummers (who had managed to get out of games by "having the painters in" AGAIN! How many periods can you have in a month?) were singing, "Nellie the elephant packed her bags and said goodbye to the circus." Then the bell went and the Bummers slouched off.

After they'd gone I gave P. Green her silly specs. She would have been in the shower rooms for the rest of her life otherwise. I hope she doesn't think that makes me her mate.

My bedroom
6:00 p.m.

No phonecall from SG. I wonder what Wet Lindsay means about using her charm on him? What kind of charm do owls have? Perhaps she will lay him an egg.

OhGodohGod. I'm getting the heebie-jeebies about my Red Herring extravaganza. How do I keep him as a herring without snogging him?

In *Bliss* in the letters page there's a letter from a girl called Sandy. She didn't really like a boy and was just using him to get off with someone else. Unfortunately the advice from Agony Jane was not "Carry on and good luck to you". The advice was "You are a really horrible girl, Sandy. You will never have a happy life, you cow." (Well, it didn't exactly say it in those words but that is what the gist and nub was.)

Decided to put the squeaking dolphins on and do some calming yoga. I used to be quite good at doing the sun salute last term until Miss Stamp surprised me in the gym with my bottom sticking up in the air.

Mmmmmm – much much better. All soothing and flowing. Lalalalala. Lift your arms up to worship the sun... breathe in... hhmmmmmmm, then put your arms down to the floor like in "we are not worth" in football... aahhh, breathe out. Much calmer. Then swing to the right and swing to the left.

That's funny... if I turned to the right, then the left, a funny noise came out of me. Like a sort of wheezy noise. Could it be the dolphins? I didn't know they did wheezing.

Turned the tape off.

Now then, to the right, to the left. Oh no. Wheeze wheeze. If I went really fast from the right to the left I could hear wheeze wheeze wheeze. Which is not what you want.

It was really quite loud. Wheeze wheeze.

I'd probably caught TB from being made to do swimming in freezing conditions.

Mum came in with a cup of tea for me (without knocking, naturally) and caught me doing my wheezing movements. She said, "Are you dancing?" and I said, "No I'm not, I'm wheezing. I think I may have caught TB. It's not as if I'm in tiptop physical condition, with the kind of diet that we live on."

She said, "Don't be so silly, what is the matter?"

I didn't want her to listen to my wheezing but I had really freaked myself out. I let her listen. Side to side, wheeze wheeze.

She looked worried. (Probably thinking she would be chastised by the local press for child abuse and neglect.) She said, "Look, I think maybe we should pop up to the surgery and see George Cloon— er... the doctor. Get your coat."

Before I could protest she grabbed Libby and we were out of the door. As she started the car I said, "Look Mum, perhaps if I had a warm bath and you made me a nourishing stew..."

The next thing I knew I was in the doctors' waiting room. It was full of the elderly mad, all coughing. If I wasn't sick now I was soon going to be.

Libby got up on a table to do a little dance for everyone. It must have been something she had learned at kindergarten. It seemed to be sung to "Pop Goes the Weasel".

Libby sang (loudly and with a lot of actions), "Ha ha pag of trifle atishoo atishoo all fall down." The finale was her throwing up her dress and pulling down her panties.

Mum hadn't expected that bit. Who could? There was a lot of muttering from the very old. One woman said, "Disgusting!" which was a bit rich coming from someone wearing a balaclava.

Eventually we got to see the doc. Mum practically threw herself through the surgery door and I was left dragging Libby because she wanted to do an encore.

Mum said, "Oh, hello, it's us again!" in a really odd girlie voice. When I had got Libby's knickers back on I looked at the doctor. He was quite fit-looking actually, not at all the surly red-faced madman that normally treated us. There was a bit of the young George Clooney about this one.

He smiled (ummm) and said, "Yes, hello again, Connie. (Connie!) Hello, Libby." Libby gave him one of her very mad smiles.

Then he looked at me. I gave him my attractive half smile. (Curved lips but no teeth, nose snugly pulled in.)

He said, "And this must be Georgia. What can I do for you?"

Mum said, "Tell the doctor, Gee."

Reluctantly I said, "Well, when I do this..." (and I did the side to side thing), "...a wheezy noise comes out of me."

The doctor said, "Does it happen any other time?"

I said, "Er... no."

And he said, "Only when you go from side to side?"

And I said, "Yes."

And he said, "Well, I wouldn't go from side to side, then." And that was it.

Thanks a lot. All that money we (well, my parents) paid in taxes for his medical training not gone to waste, then!! He smiled at me, "When you move like that you force the air out of your lungs and it makes a sort of noise. That's all. They're just like bellows, really."

I felt like a fool. Two fools. It was Mum's fault for making me go. And she just hung around the doctor for AGES. Making conversation. Telling him she was learning salsa dancing. Did he like dancing? Etc. She kept saying, "Oh, I mustn't keep you," and then going on and on. It was only when the nurse knocked on the door and said one of the pensioners had fallen off their chair that Mum pulled herself together.

It was so embarrassing; Mum was practically dribbling.

She has zero pride. Now that my life was not in danger I noticed that even in the emergency of getting me to the doctor she had managed to squeeze herself into a tight top. You could see she was thrusting her "danger to shippings" at him. In a way, and I never thought I would say this, it will be quite a relief when Vati comes home.

In the car going home she said, "He's nice, isn't he?"

I said, "Mum, honestly, have a bit of dignity. You have made your life choice and the large Portly One is on his way home in a fortnight. It is not a good idea to risk your marriage, and also incidentally make yourself a laughing stock this late on in life."

She said, "Georgia, I really don't know what you are talking about."

She does though.

Do I have to worry about every bloody single thing round this place? When do I get a chance to be a selfish teenager? Jas's mum and dad have aprons and sheds, why do I have to have Mr and Mrs "We've Got Lives of Our Own" as parents?

Thursday October 7th

11:30 a.m.

The Bummer Twins have both got their knickers in a twist. They saw Nauseating P. Green coming out of a classroom, talking to Wet Lindsay. P. Green was probably telling her something about hamster feed. But the Bummers are saying she is a snitcher because they got done for knocking off school the other day. They call Nauseating P. Green "Snitcher the Elephant" now. They stole her *Hamsters Weekly*. I thought she was going to cry which would have been horrific.

Rosie sent me a note in Maths; it said, I am an equilateral triangle.

I wrote back and said, Does that mean all your angles are equal? and she wrote, I don't know, I'm a triangle.

I looked over at her and pushed my nose back like a pig. She did the same thing back. We could while away the hours much more amusingly if we could sit together.

I said that to Slim when she split us up last term. I said, "Miss Simpson, it is a well-known fact that if friends sit together they are encouraged to do more work." But she just shook in such a jelloid way I thought her chins would drop off.

She said, "The last time you two sat together, you set the locusts free in the Biology lab."

Oh honestly, not only has she got legs like an elephant, she has got a memory like one. How many times did we have to explain it was an accident? No one could have imagined they would eat Mr Attwood's spare overalls.

It is RE in a couple of hours so I will be able to have a decent chat to my mates instead of wasting time learning about stuff.

RE
1:30 p.m.

Rosie bunked off, she said she was going to the pictures with Sven. It must be nice to have a boyfriend, even if it was Sven. Oh well, ho hum, pig's bum. While Miss Wilson raved on and hitched up her sad tights I chatted to Jas. She wasn't officially speaking to me because of the veggie business, but I put my arm round her every time I went near her. In the end, to stop me and also to avoid more lezzie rumours, she forgave me (ish).

I said, "My vati is back on the nineteenth."

"Are you glad?"

"No, Jas, I said my vati is back on the nineteenth."

"I like my dad."

"Yes, but your dad is normal. He's got a shed. He does DIY. He fixed your bike. When my vati tried to fix my bike his hand got stuck in the spokes. We had to walk to casualty. I don't see why I had to go with him, everyone was calling out in the streets. And they weren't calling out 'What a brilliant dad you've got!'"

3:45 p.m.
I've managed not to think about meeting Dave all day. I am a bit nervous, though.

7:30 p.m.
In my bedroom. I've got my head under my pillow. This house is like a mental institution. In the front room Uncle Eddie and Mum are practising salsa. He turned up on his motorbike with a crate of wine. First of all he came snooping up to my room and opened my door (I don't know why we don't just take it off its hinges and leave it at that). I think he must have already had one crate of wine because he had a tennis racket he was pretending to play as a guitar and he said, "Georgia, this is a little song entitled, 'Get off the stove, Grandad, you're too old to ride the range'," then he laughed like King Loon and went off downstairs singing, "Agadoo doo dooo."

174

Honestly, what planet do these people live on? And why isn't it further away? Libby is in the airing cupboard with Angus. She says they are playing doctors and nurses.

11:00 p.m.
Does anyone care what happens to me?

I've got to meet Dave the L. tomorrow and somehow cover up the fact that I have a broken heart. I must be glittering and glamorous and brave.

I could hear Mum and Uncle Eddie giggling. I called down, "Mum... Libby is still in the airing cupboard if you were wondering, which I don't suppose you were as you are busy drinking and carrying on, and so on."

I wondered if I should confide in Uncle Eddie about Mum and George Clooney. Maybe he could have a word with her? Then I heard him coming upstairs again. He popped his very bald head round my door, the light glancing off it almost blinded me, and he said, "We can go and meet your dad on my motorbike if you like!!"

Yeah, in your dreams, oh mad bald one.

Friday October 8th
4:00 p.m.

The Fab Gang came round and we hung around in my room, listening to the Top 20. We were discussing Operation Red Herring. Well me and Mabs, Rosie, Jools and Ellen were, Jas wasn't there. Too busy waiting for her "boyfriend" to come home to worry about her very best pal in the world, who would never dream of putting boys first.

Ellen said, "OK, this is the plan. Say to the herring you have to be home by nine thirty because you are grounded for staying out too late."

I said, "Yes, that's good because it makes me seem sort of like dangerous and groovy but it also means I can get away if I need to. Good thinking, Batwoman."

Ellen went on, "And me and the rest of the gang will sort of be around the park any time things might be getting heavy."

I said, "Yeah. Because that is like double cool... almost with knobs. It means I have loads of mates that I just casually bump into at every whiff and woo AND it will stop any hanky panky in the snogging department."

Rosie said, "Exactamondo. Let's dance!"

And we did mad dancing to calm ourselves down.

176

7:00 p.m.

Met Dave the L. in the park. I went for casual glamour: leopard-skin top (fake, because otherwise Angus would have followed me thinking he'd made a new big mate) and jeans and leather jacket. It was a bit awkward at first. You know, like a first date. He is quite a good-looking bloke if you like red herrings. He said, "Hi, gorgeous," which I think is nice. I admire honesty.

He told me he wanted to be a stand-up comedian when he leaves school and I said, "You should have my life, that would give you lots of material."

He laughed. It was funny but I didn't feel nervous, not like with SG. I didn't say I wanted to be a vet or anything. I very nearly made sense.

As we walked along chatting our arms sort of brushed against each other a couple of times. I didn't mind and he's got a nice crinkly smile. But then he grabbed hold of my hand. Uh-oh. Hanky panky. Also he is slightly smaller than me and I had to do the bendy knee business so I could be more his height. I don't know what it is about boys these days but they seem on the small side. Or perhaps I am growing. Oh no. That might be it. I might only be half the size I am going to be. I might turn out to be a female Sven and that might be God's punishment for me turning Buddhist. Anyway, I lolloped along as best I could, trying not to be like an orang-utan. But, oh *sacré bleu* and *merde*, then Dave pulled me round to face him and took hold of my other hand. I had to lift up my shoulders so that I didn't have excess arm. I felt like that woman in *The Sound of Music*, you know, Julie Thing. Surely he wasn't going to start dancing round with me? Nooooo, he wasn't. He was going to kiss me!! Oh no, this wasn't in the Herring plan... Where were all my so-called mates???

As he looked at me and started to bring his face closer I said really quickly, "Have you noticed how when you go from side to side there is this sort of wheezing noise?"

But I only got to "Ha..." when he put his mouth on mine. I could have bitten through my tongue. I kept my eyes open because I thought that wouldn't be like a real kiss. But it made me go cross-eyed so I closed them. It was, in fact, quite a nice kiss. (But what do I know? I've only ever been with SG, a whelk boy and BG (Mark) who had such a huge gob that no experience with him can be counted normal. You've just got to be glad to escape without being eaten.)

My room
Thinking
11:00 p.m.

My so-called mates arrived at last. They gave us both a bit of a start, leaping out from behind a tree. Also if Rosie is thinking of taking up drama I would advise her against it. She said, "Oh hello, Georgia. It's YOU!!! What on EARTH are you doing here. I thought you were GROUNDED?" But she said it like somebody had hit her on the head with a mallet (which, incidentally, somebody should do).

11:30 p.m.

Hmmm. I am in a state of confusosity. I'd rate him as seven and a half as a kisser. Maybe even eight. He didn't do much varying pressure and his tongue work was a bit like a little snake. On the other hand he didn't do any sucking (like whelk boy) and there was no crashing of teeth. Or dribbling, which is never acceptable. He did nibble my lower lip a bit, which I must tell the gang about because it isn't on our list. It was quite nice. I might try doing it myself. When I retrap the SG.

Midnight
Also he didn't rest his hand on my basooma, which is a plus.

12:30 a.m.
Maybe he didn't rest his hand there because he thought he might never find it again? I wonder if my basoomas are still growing?

12:32 a.m.
Terrible news!! I can fit a pencil case underneath my basooma and it actually stays there for a second!!

I feel all hot and weird. Still, what else is new?

Saturday October 9th
11:50 a.m.
Angus is in love!!! Honestly. With Mr and Mrs Across the Road's Burmese pedigree cat Naomi. (I call her that, they call her Little-Brook-Running-up-a-Tree-With-a-Sausage-up-its-Bottom Sun Li the Third, or something foreign.) I saw Angus on their wall, giving Naomi a vole he'd killed. He was parading up and down sticking his bottom up in the air and waggling his tail about. Disgusting, really. Especially as he

had a clinker hanging out of his bum-oley. Cats think that is attractive. So does Libbs.

Mr and Mrs Across the Road didn't seem too thrilled by his attentions. In fact, they threw stones at him. They are going to have to try a lot harder than that, he was brought up having bricks thrown at him. They should try a bazooka.

My room
2:30 p.m.
I must find some calm. I've got an instruction booklet on Buddhism from the library. Miss Wilson, who doubles as sad librarian, is beside herself with pleasure – she thinks I am taking religion seriously due to her excellent teaching. Sad really. She'll want me to go round for coffee at her house soon. I might go and ask her where she buys her tights. The book is called *Buddhism for the Stupid*. No, it's not really, but it should be.

Good grief. It's so boring. It's just all about world peace and so on, which is OK but you would think I could do that later. Once I was happy. And had got what I wanted.

4:00 p.m.
Jas turned up. She was really mopey like a cod.

"I got all ready for Tom to come home and then he called up from Birmingham and said he was going to stay on for a few more days. He says that he likes Birmingham and has got some great new mates."

I was thinking, Oh, good grief! As if I haven't got enough to worry about without having Hunky and Po in trouble. But I didn't say anything.

Jas moaned on: "He didn't used to like going out with mates, he used to like being with me."

I said wisely: "Remember he is a Jennings boy. He is the same as Robbie. Remember the elastic band thing, Jas... let him have his space. In fact, why don't you say you think you should have a break from each other for a bit? You know, to sort of find yourselves."

Jas said, "I know where he is, he is in Birmingham."

It's easier chatting to Angus. I kept on, though. "Don't be silly, Po! Anyway, I want to talk to you about Buddha. Do you know what Buddha says?"

"Didn't he say quite a lot?"

"Yes, but he said, 'When a crow finds a dying snake, it behaves as if it were an eagle. When I see myself as a victim I am hurt by trifling failures.'"

There was a silence and Jas started fiddling around with her fringe.

"Do you see?"

"Er... what has that got to do with Tom? He's not an eagle."

Honestly she is so dim. I explained, as patiently as I could, "It means, if you think your life is poo it will be."

"Well why didn't he say that?"

"Because a) he is Buddha and b) they do not have poo in Buddhaland."

5:30 p.m.
Phone rang. Mum yelled up, "Gee, it's for you... boyfriend."

Honestly, I could kill her. I went and answered the phone and sat down on a stool. It was Dave the Laugh. He said, "Hello, Gorge. I had a great time last night. I've just about recovered from meeting your mates. What are you up to?"

As I was chatting to him Libby came humming into the hall. She wanted to get up on to my knee.

I said, "Libbs, I'm on the phone, go find Angus to play with."

She gave me her frowniest look. "NO... UP!!! NOW!!!

BAD, BAD BOY." And she started spitting at me so I had to let her on my knee. Before I could stop her she was "talking" down the phone. "Hello, mister man. Grrrrrrr. Three bag pool, three bag pool."

Oh God. I struggled to get the phone off her and then she shouted, "Georgie has got a THERY big SPOT! Hahahahahaha."

I grabbed the phone back and put Libby on the floor. "Sorry about that, Dave, my little sister has... er... just learned to talk and, er she must have... er..."

Libby was singing, "Georgie's got a THERY big spot, lalalalala, THERY, THERY big spot... ON HER BOT... ON HER BOTTY."

6:00 p.m.
She's right, actually. How can you get spots on your bottom? I must have more vitamin C.

6:05 p.m.
Me and Jas chomping on bananas. Jas said, "Save the skins because they make really good face masks."

6:30 p.m.

As usual Jas is completely wrong. We washed off the banana on our faces; it felt disgusting.

I said, "I'm meeting Dave again tomorrow. He seems to really like me."

Jas was busy picking bits of banana out of her hair. "Does he? Why?"

"I don't know, he just does."

Bed
11:00 p.m.

Dave doesn't make my legs go jelloid and that is the point, isn't it? If a boy doesn't make you go jelloid you may as well be with your girlie mates... or boy mates that you are just mates with and no snogging involved.

11:30 p.m.

Oh, I don't know.

Midnight

Angus still on the wall looking down at Naomi the Burmese

sex kitten. She is rubbing herself against the wall, the little minx. I know what she feels like.

I wonder what the Sex God is doing now.

What shall I do about Dave?

1:00 a.m.

I really would truly prefer to put my head into a bag of eels than kiss Wet Lindsay.

1:15 a.m.

Sex God did take the bull by the nostrils and dump Wet Lindsay when he found true love (me). Even if he did then dump me.

1:30 a.m.

He was true to his feelings. Even though it upset Owlie he dumped her because it was the right thing to do (and it is always the right thing to do to dump Owlie).

Sunday October 10th
10:00 p.m.

Dave the L. turned up at my door earlier, wearing a false

moustache. He actually is quite a laugh. We went to the pictures and snogged again. He must be a bit surprised that my mates pop up every time we go anywhere. When Rosie put her head over the back of us in the pictures and said, "GEORGIA!!! HOW AMAZING!! What are you doing here?!!!" I thought he'd swallow his ice cream whole.

Monday October 11th
School
8:30 a.m.

I met Jas on the way to school. She was trailing her rucky along as we walked. I said, "Dave sent me a card today, it said, *Merry one week anniversary, gorgeous. Lots of love, D, kiss, kiss, kiss.*"

She didn't say anything. I said, "Jas, what are you doing?"

She was all pale, I noticed.

"I haven't heard from Tom and I tried to ring him and he was out."

"Ah yes, well."

"You said I should say, 'Have your own space, Tom'."

"Yes, well..."

"And now he's got loads of space."

"Ah yes."

"And so have I."

"Yes…"

"But I don't want it."

Oh good grief. I'm not going to be an agony aunt if all people do is moan on all the time.

Last bell
3:50 p.m.

Jas, Jools, Ellen, Rosie and me were lurking near the science block, hiding from the Gestapo (Hawkeye) who wants to ask me about the lunchbox beret idea. Everyone has been doing it. Slim told us not to be so silly; she said in assembly, "You are making a mockery of the school's good name in the community."

Anyway, we have taken her advice to heart and we are going to have a "blind day" instead. After last bell we went to the alleyway in between the Science block and main school, waiting for an opportunity to dash out of the gates when Hawkeye was not looking. We all had our lunchpack-berets on apart from old spoilsport knickers Jas.

Rosie said, "On the blind day next Wednesday the deal is we all shut our eyes for the whole morning and have to have minders that guide us around. From lesson to lesson."

I said, "Wait a minute, we have sports on Wednesday, it's hockey. That will be a laugh."

Jas said gloomily – she had been an unlaugh all day – "Hawkeye will stop us, with detention and so on."

Rosie said, "No, because we will explain that we are being sponsored and are doing it so that we will have a better understanding of the poorly-sighted."

That's when we saw something awful. The SG drove up to the school gates in his car and Wet Lindsay ran out and got in!

7:00 p.m.

In a way I feel free. If SG chooses Owlie over me then he is the loser. So be it. That is the Buddhist way. Omm. I will not be the crow finding the snake or whatever it found. Who cares? It's only a crow.

8:00 p.m.

I need a break from being a Buddhist for a minute. POOO!!! DOUBLE *MERDE*!!! Life really is a pooburger.

9:00 p.m.

Mum came in for a "chat".

"Dad's home in a week."

"Still time for a few serious medical complaints, then."

"What do you mean?"

"You and Doctor Clooney."

"Georgia, you're mad."

"Am I?"

"Look, all it is is that I think he's quite good-looking."

"Well that's because you are comparing him to Dad."

"Don't be rude."

"I'm not, I'm being factual."

"Anyway, you needn't worry, it's just innocent flirting."

"Yes it is for you but what if Doctor Clooney really likes you? And what about if he will be really upset if he finds out you are just toying with him? Like a toying person?"

She went off looking all worried. Good. That's two of us all worried and guilty. And confused.

9:30 p.m.

Dave phoned. He said, "I just called to say I really like you. Night-night."

Good grief.

I wonder if all heartless babe magnets feel guilty?

Tuesday October 12th
Hockey pitch
2:30 p.m.

Hockey match against boring old Hollingbury College. They really do think they are cool, but sadly they are about to find out that they are not.

I had a sneaky look in their changing room when I pretended to be fastening up my boots. It was a nightmare of thongs. I noticed Miss Stamp busily popping in and out, saying things like, "Don't mind me, I was just wondering if you had enough towels."

She was all red and keen. Running on the spot, and so on. Very alarming if you're not used to it. I noticed quite a few of the Hollingbury girls were rushing off into the loos when she came in. They were getting a bit jittery. So I used sporting tactics. I said, "Miss Stamp, I wonder if the

Hollingbury team would appreciate a bit of physio after the match. You know, if they had any little knocks or anything you could offer to... er... treat them yourself. Use those magic healing hands."

Adolfa was a bit suspicious. But she couldn't figure out my angle. I heard her go back into their changing room and say something about treatment. All of the Hollingbury girls shot out of the door and on to the pitch. Ah good, a nervous team, desperate not to get injured!! Result!!!

It's very nippy noodles. I've got three pairs of knickers on. I probably look like Nauseating P. Green from the back... or Slim. Still, better a fat bum than a numb bum. There is a little crowd supporting us, most of my mates actually. Although not Jas, she wasn't at school today. I hope she has not gone all weird because of Tom.

The slimiest wet weed who shall remain nameless (Lindsay) is captain of the team. Erlack... well I will not do anything that she says. In our pre-match talk she said, "So remember to watch me for instruction, and when you get into any kind of shooting position, watch for me to come and take on the shot."

Oh yeah, dream on, wet and weedy one. With a bit of

luck someone will knock her stick insect legs from under her. I am not saying I want her to be badly injured, just badly enough that she has to go away to a convalescent hospital somewhere (Mars) for a year or two. Thank you, Buddha. (You can see how I am not taking poo lying down.)

2:50 p.m.
Cracking match. I am playing a stormer, even if I say so myself. Zipping up and down the pitch, hitting the ball up to the forwards. Excellent passing!! I'm like David Beckham apart from the hockey stick and skirt and three pairs of huge knickers. Although who knows? Posh Spice may insist he wears sensible snug knickers in the winter time. She is a very caring person. But quite thin.

Half-time
No score
3:15 p.m.
Rosie, Ellen, Jools and Mabs are like cheerleaders. They have made up this song which goes, "One – two – three – four – go, Georgia, go!"

I said to them as I came off, "It doesn't rhyme," and Ellen said, "Well, it's too nippy noodles."

❤ 193

Brrr. She's right. I went into the loos to run my hands under the hot water tap. Oh no, the Bummer Twins had got Nauseating P. Green cornered in the changing rooms. She was blubbing. They didn't even look round when I came in. Jackie said, "So, Snitcher, what did you tell Lindsay about us knocking off school?"

Nauseating P. Green was trembling like a huge jelly elephant. "I... I... didn't say... anything..."

I thought I should shout at her, to help, "Tell them about your hamsters, P. Green, that will bore them to death and you can run off." But I looked at Jackie's big arms and thought I wouldn't bother.

As I was going out again the Bummers started shoving P. Green against the loo doors. Oh bum, bum.

Alison said, "We don't like snitchers... do we, Georgia?"

I said, "Oh, they're all right, I—"

Jackie shoved P. Green so hard that her glasses flew off. That did it. I could no longer be the Bummer Twins' armchair. I said, "Leave her alone now."

Jackie looked at me. "Oh yeah, big nose, what are you going to do about it?"

I said, "I'm going to appeal to your niceness."

She laughed and said, "Dream on, Ringo."

I said, "Yes, I thought that might not work, so this is plan two."

Actually there wasn't a plan two. I didn't know what I was doing. I was like a thing possessed. I leaped over to them and grabbed Jackie's fag packet out of her hand. Then I ran into the loos with it and held it over the toilet. I yelled, "Let her go or the fags get it!"

Jackie was truly worried then and had a sort of reflex action to save her packet of fags. Alison came towards me as well, leaving Nauseating P. Green trembling by herself. I shouted, "Run like the wind, P. Green!!!"

She picked up her glasses and just stood there, blinking like a porky rabbit caught in a car's headlights. Good grief! I tried to give her confidence. "Well, not like the wind, then, but shuffle off as fast as you can."

Eventually she went off and I was left to face the Bummers. I charged past them shouting, "Uurgghhhhgghhh!", that well-known Buddhist warrior chant. I chucked the fags out of the packet on to the floor. When I looked back as I dashed out of the door they were scrabbling around picking them up. I raced out on to the pitch for the second half to a big cheer from the

Ace Crew. I thought I may as well enjoy the game because the Bummers would be killing me immediately after it was over.

I noticed there were a few boys gathered at the opposite end of the pitch. One of them cheered when I ran on. Probably Foxwood lads. They sort of appeared any time there was the least hint of knicker flashing. Or nunga-nunga wobbling. I don't know how they knew, or had found out we were playing today. Probably Elvis Attwood got on the tom-toms in his hut and drummed out a message to let them know there was a match on. He was lurking around pretending to be busy, wheeling his wheelbarrow. There was never anything in it. Old Pervy Trousers. Anyway, let the lads look at my nunga-nungas if they wanted! Let my nostrils flare free. Let my waddly bottom waddle, what did I care??? I was going to be dead anyway when the Bummers got hold of me.

4:10 p.m.
Victory! Victory!!!!! We won one-nil.

It was a close match considering we were playing such a bunch of wets. One of their team blubbed when I accidentally hit her on the shin with my stick. I wonder if all the times I have been savaged by Angus have made me immune to pain? Anyway, it was a nil draw until the last few minutes. I raced up the wing and found myself in the opposition's penalty area. The Ace Crew were going, "Georgia Georgia!!" And then our so-called captain Wet Lindsay shouted from the left side, "Pass it to me, number eight!"

You know like in the movies when everything slows down and it's in slow motion? Well, I had that. I saw Owlie's face and her thin stupid legs and I thought, Hahahahahahaha! (Only really, really slowly.)

I kept the ball myself and raced for goal with it. I dribbled past one opposition player, then another. Tripped. Picked myself up, nipped the ball through someone's legs. The crowd were cheering me on. They were going BERSERK!! Then there was the goalkeeper. Good grief, she was a giant!!! But I feinted to one side of her and got past. Then there was just the open goal. I whacked the ball and scored!!!... just as Lindsay tackled me savagely from behind.

4:30 p.m.
Wet Lindsay tried to pretend that she had been "helping" me. Huh. Very likely... not.

Miss Stamp wanted Elvis to carry me to the sick bay but he said he had an old war wound and brought his wheelbarrow out on to the pitch. He said, "Get in. One of your mates will have to wheel it because I hurt my back serving this country."

Oh yeah. I said to Jools, "His back has probably seized up because he sits on his bottom all day."

Rosie wheeled me to the sick bay but I still couldn't walk even after the sadistic Adolfa Stamp had strapped up my ankle. While she was kneeling down in front of me bandaging it all my so-called mates were behind her doing pretend snogging. The Hollingbury girls didn't even bother to get changed, they just shook hands really quickly and got on their coach.

I hopped about a bit after I was strapped up but it was aggers. In the end Elvis said reluctantly that Rosie and Ellen and Jools could push me home in the wheelbarrow. Cheers, thanks a lot.

Elvis went grumbling back to his hut, saying, "Make sure you bring it back tomorrow... it's my own private equipment and shouldn't by rights be used for school business."

His own private wheelbarrow. How sad is that? Sensationally sad, that's how.

We set off, wheeling along. It wasn't very comfortable in

the barrow and there was the suggestion of something brownish in one of the corners. But I was being all brave and heroic as I was the heroine of the hockey universe. And attractively modest. For a genius.

When we got to the school gates Dave the Laugh was there!!! He had been one of the lads at the match!!! He has seen my gigantic bottom bobbling around on the pitch. Closely following my gigantic schnozzle, bobbling around, OhmyGodohmyGodohmyGod.

He was laughing like a loon as we squeaked up to him in Elvis's wheelbarrow. Then he got down on his knees and was salaaming and chanting "We are not worthy" to me.

He said to Rosie and Ellen and Jools, "Let me push the genius home." And as he pushed me along he sang that really crap song by that band that Dad thinks he looks like the drummer from – Queen. The song was "We are the Champions". The Fab Gang joined in really loudly. Everyone was looking as us as we went down the High Street. I don't suppose shoppers often saw anyone in a wheelbarrow. They probably had very narrow lives and travelled around by car. Or moped.

Dave the L. kissed me when he left me at my gate! In

front of everyone! And he said, "Bye-bye, beautiful. See you soon. Let me know how the ankle is. I'll bring you pressies."

When he'd gone the girls went, "Aaaahhh."

Ellen said, "He really is quite cool-looking. Has he done that nibbling thing again? I quite fancy the sound of that."

But he is just a herring. We must not forget this.

6:15 p.m.

Mum was quite literally ecstatic about my ankle. She just left me in the wheelbarrow outside the front door and got on the blower immediately. I could hear her talking to the doctors' receptionist.

"Yes, it really does seem quite bad. No, no, she really can't walk at all. Yes, well thank you."

Libby came trailing out with scuba-diving Barbie and got in the wheelbarrow with me. She gave me a big kiss. Don't get me wrong, I love my sister, but I wish she would wipe her nose occasionally. When she kisses me she leaves green snot all over my cheek.

Mum came outside and said, "The doctor will pop round after surgery, Gee. Will you just lend me your mascara? I've run out."

I said, "Huh, it's just one-way traffic in this house... if it was me, if the shoe was on the other boot, if I said, 'Mum, can I just borrow...'"

She wasn't listening. She called from indoors, "Hurry up, love, just get me it."

I yelled, "I can't walk, Mum! That is why the doctor is coming to see me. That's why I came home in a wheelbarrow."

"You don't have to walk, just hop out of the barrow and up the stairs and get the mascara."

Hop hop, agony agony, hop hop.

Why was I hopping around getting things for my mother who only wanted them so that she could make a fool of my father? (The answer to that question is I didn't want her poking around in my room. She might come across a few things that weren't strictly mine, things that in a word were – er – hers.)

I hopped into her bedroom and said, "It is pathetic and sad. You are trying to get off with a young doctor and my poor vati is coming home to a – a – facsimile of a sham!"

She just tutted and went on primping. She said, "The trouble with you is that trivial things are really serious to you, and stuff you should care about that is serious, you don't."

I said, hobbling off, "Oh very wise. Is that why you are

stuffing yourself into things that are quite clearly made for people a) smaller than you and b) several centuries younger than you?"

She threw the hairbrush at me. That's nice behaviour, isn't it? Attacking a cripple.

7:00 p.m.

Doctor Home-wrecker arrived. He strapped up my ankle again and gave me painkillers. I said, "I suppose that is my hockey career over. Do you think that perhaps I have weak ankles because of my diet?"

He laughed. He had a good laugh, actually.

Mum said, "Can I get you a coffee, John?"

John? John? Where did that come from?

Mum went off into the kitchen and I heard her say, "Take Angus out of the fridge, Libbs."

"He likes it."

"He's eaten all the butter."

"Teehhheeeeeheeee."

7:15 p.m.

I hobbled off to my room and played moody music really

loudly as a hint. It was ages before the door slammed. I looked out of my bedroom window. I could see John going off in his quite cool car.

7:45 p.m.
Lying on my bed of pain. Well, it would be if I could feel my ankle.

Mum popped her head round the door. She was all flushed. "How is the ankle?"

I said, "Fine if you like red-hot pokers being stabbed in you."

"That's my little soldier." She was humming.

Brilliant, a week before my dad gets back my mum starts a torrid affair with a doctor.

8:00 p.m.
Mind you, I would get tiptop medical priority.

8:30 p.m.
He might be able to get me a good deal on my nose job.

9:00 p.m.
I must get revenge on Wet Lindsay.

10:00 p.m.

I wonder how the Bummers will kill me?

10:10 p.m.

Why is the Herring so nice to me? What is wrong with him?

Wednesday October 13th
School
8:30 a.m.

Mum made me hobble to school. Unbelievable. She said a bad ankle didn't stop me learning things. I tried to explain to Mum that it would be just a question of hobbling in to be killed by the Bummer Twins, but she wasn't interested.

I made Jas wheel the wheelbarrow as I hopped along with a crutch. The Foxwood lads had a field day with us, shouting, "Where's your parrot?" and so on.

Jas had perked up enough to say, "I wonder how the Bummers will kill you?"

She sounded quite interested. She's only cheered up because Tom is coming home.

I managed to keep out of the Bummers' way for the

morning but eventually at lunchtime the fatal moment came. The Bummers cornered me in the loos. I tried to hobble off but they blocked the doorway. Here we go. Well at least death would solve the Dave the Laugh situation. Jackie just looked at me. She said, "Fancy a fag?"

What were they going to do, ritually set fire to me?

Jackie put a fag in my mouth and Alison lit it. Jackie said, "Cool," and Alison said, "Good call." And then they just went out.

What in the name of pantyhose did that mean? Why hadn't they duffed me up?

I hobbled over to the mirror to see what I looked like smoking. Quite cool, actually. I sucked my nose in. I definitely looked a bit Italian.

Out of the corner of my mouth I said, "*Ciao, bella.*"

But sadly smoke went up my nose and I had a coughing extravaganza.

I can't believe life. As I was having my coughing fit Lindsay walked in and booked me for smoking in the loos. I saw the Bummer Twins sniggering in the corridor.

Great. Stacking gym mats for the rest of the term. Elvis passed by and saw me hobbling and heaving mats around. He laughed.

4:00 p.m.

Left school limping along next to Jas. I think it's quite attractive if you like Long John Silver. I said to Jas, "You know, I think I am going to give up on boys altogether – tell Dave the Laugh it's over, forget the Sex God and just concentrate on lessons and so on. I might ask Herr Kamyer to give me extra tuition."

"He'd have a spasm to end all spasms if you did."

I said, "I think I might be over the Sex God anyway. When I saw him pick up Owlie in his car, that did it for me. Anyone who can go out with Wet Lindsay, with her stupid no forehead and sticky insect legs, and... er..."

"Goggly eyes?"

"Yeah, goggly eyes. Anyone who can do that has got something very wrong with them. You know, if he asked me out now I would say n–ung."

I meant to say "no" but that was when I saw him leaning against his car. The Sex God. Oh don't tell me he was waiting for gorgeous (not) Wet Lindsay. Pathetic. *Très* pathetic and *très très* sad.

I hobbled past him. He wasn't so very gorgey. Well actually, yes, he was. He was a Sex God. Really. He looked me straight in the eyes and I went completely jelloid. In fact, my other leg nearly gave way. He half-smiled and I remembered what it was like to be attached to his mouth. Somehow I kept hobbling. We'd got past him and I was feeling all shaky when he called after us, "Georgia, can I talk to you for a minute?"

OhmyGodohmyGod. Was this an elastic band moment? Jas was just goosegogging at my side. I said, "You walk on, Jas, I'll catch you up."

She said, "Oh it's OK, I'm not in any hurry. Anyway, you might fall over and lie for ages with no one to help you. Like a tortoise on its back or—"

I opened my eyes really wide at Jas and raised my eyebrows. After about forty years she got it and walked on.

Robbie said, "Look, I know I'm probably the last person you want to talk to, but... well... I'd just like to tell you something... I'm really, really sorry about what happened between us... I handled it really badly, I know. She, you know, Lindsay, just was like, so upset, and you were so young and I couldn't... I didn't know what else to do. I thought I'd be going away soon and that would just sort things out... but then I was at the match..."

God, was there anyone in the universe who hadn't seen my huge wobbly bottom and enormous conk bobbling around the hockey pitch?

SG was going on in his really sexy voice, "...and I saw how Lindsay deliberately hurt you... and I... I'm sorry. I've caused a lot of trouble and you're a really nice kid... Look, I'll..."

Then I heard, "Robbie!!"

Wet Lindsay was walking over towards where we were and I just couldn't handle any more. I hobbled off.

5:00 p.m.

OhGodohGodohGod. I love him, I love him.

He thinks I am a kid.

It's all a facsimile of a sham.

And in tins.

And pants.

And pingy pongos.

And *merde*.

He was at the match. He saw my giganticus pantibus.

But he still spoke to me.

Perhaps Jas is not as mad as she seems. Perhaps big knickers are boy magnets?

Oh I don't know.

Why does he still make me go jelloid?

6:00 p.m.

Dave the Laugh had left me a card at home which said, *One-legged girls are a push-over. Love Dave xxxxxx* And some chocolates. Oh GODDDDDDD!!!!

Saturday October 16th

11:00 a.m.

I am a horrible person. I have dumped Dave. I had to. It was really double poo. I thought he was going to cry. He turned up at my house with some flowers because of my injury. He is so sweet and it didn't seem fair to lead him on. I explained that he had only really been a red herring.

2:30 p.m.

Phoned Jas.

"He said I was a user and, er... something else..."

"Was it 'selfish'?"

"No."

"The crappest person in humanity?"

"No."

"Really horrible and like a wormey..."

"Jas, shut up."

In bed
8:00 p.m.

Am I really horrible? Perhaps I am one of those people who don't really feel things properly, like Madonna.

10:00 p.m.

Personally I think I have shown great maturiosity and wisdomosity.

11:00 p.m.

Dave will some day thank me for this.

Midnight

Angus still on top of the wall across the road. Looking down at his beloved Naomi in her enclosure. He too is disappointed in love.

3:00 a.m.

Libby came in all sleepy. She said, "Move." And climbed in with the usual accoutrements – Barbie, Charlie Horse, etc. I've got about half a centimetre of bed. Marvellous. Bloody marvellous.

Monday October 18th
School
Break
2:15 p.m.

Well, at least life can't get any worse. Oh, I beg your pardon, yes it can. Raining again and cold and we have been forced outside by the Hitler Youth. I said to Wet Lindsay who was the prefect on duty, "It is against the Geneva Convention that we are forced outside in Arctic..." But she had locked the door and was sort of grinning through the window. She took off her cardigan as I was looking and wiped her forehead as if she was boiling. Oh *très amusant*, Owlie.

Jas and I wandered round to Elvis's hut to see if the old lunatic was in. If he wasn't we could sit in his hut for a bit and warm up. But oh no, there he was, reading his newspaper. Elvis had ear muffs on underneath his flat cap! Mrs Elvis must be very proud. I tapped on his little window so that I could say a friendly hello to him. But he couldn't hear because of the muffs.

I said to Jas, "As a hilarious joke I'll pretend to say something very urgent to him but I won't really be saying anything. I'll mime saying, 'Mr Attwood, my friend Jas is on fire!!!'"

211

So I went up to the hut door and I was mouthing, "Mr Attwood, my friend Jas is on fire!!!" and waving my arms wildly. In the end he took off his ear muffs, thinking that he couldn't hear me because of them. When he realised the joke he went ballisticisimus. He leaped up in a quite scary way for a one hundred and eighty-year-old man and came charging at us out of his hut. I hobbled off quite quickly. Unfortunately he didn't remember he had parked his personal wheelbarrow round the corner of his hut and did a spectacular comedy fall over it. I thought I would die laughing. Me and Jas went and bent over a wall at the back of the tennis courts.

I said to Jas, in between laughing and gasping for air. "Jas... Jas... he... he has got a flat head."

God it was funny. I had a real ache in my stomach from laughing too much.

French
3:00 p.m.
For a "treat" as it is Monday, Madame Slack taught us another French song. It was called "Sur le Pont D'Avignon". About some absolute saddos dancing about on a bridge. All I can say is that the French and me have a different idea of

having a cracking good time. Also, if I do go to French land, although I will be able to tell my new French mates that my blackbird has lost a feather, and be able to dance on bridges, I will not be able to get a filled baguette for love nor money.

At the end of the lesson Wet Lindsay came into the classroom in her role as Oberführer assistant. She smiled in a not attractive or friendly way and said, "Georgia Nicolson, report to Miss Simpson's office... NOW."

3:30 p.m.
Outside Slim's office. Oh dear. *Quelle dommage. Zut alors* and *sacré bleu* even. Now what? Unfortunately Wet Lindsay was my guard and as I looked at her I was reminded of her thongs lurking under her skirt. Going up her bum-oley. And it started me off again.

The jelloid one called me in. I was like a red-faced loon trying not to laugh. She said, "Georgia Nicolson, this is an unforgivable offence. This time you have gone too far. Berets worn like lunchpacks, noses stuck up with Selllotape, false freckles painted on noses, all these childish pranks I have put up with... Last term there was the skeleton in Mr Attwood's uniform, the locusts..."

Slim raved on and on, shaking like a gigantic jelly. "...I was hoping that you had grown up a bit. But to lure an elderly man, not in peak condition..." Blah blah blah.

It was useless my trying to explain. Mr Attwood has dislocated his shoulder and I am being held responsible. Fab. Anyway, the short and short of it is that I'm suspended for a week and Jas is on cloakroom duty. Slim said she was going to write a stiff note home to my parents telling them the circumstances. I helpfully offered to take the stiff note home myself but Slim insisted on posting it.

Hobbling home with Jas and the gang. I was a bit depressed. Again. I couldn't even be bothered putting my lunchpack-beret on.

I said to Jas, "Slim is so ludicrously suspicious! What she implied was that I would not take the note home and would pretend that I am not suspended!!"

Jas said, "Hmmm... What were you going to tell your mum after you had destroyed the note?"

"You're as bad as everyone else, Jas."

"I know, but just for interest's sake, what were you going to say?"

"I thought I might try the mysterious stomach bug. I haven't used it since last year's maths test."

4:00 P.M.
Home. Great. Life is great. Just perfectamondo. Suspended. Suspended just in time for Vati to come home and kill me. In love with a Sex God who calls me a kid. Called a heartless whatsit by Dave the Laugh. And the spot on my bum is like a boil. I wonder what Buddha would do now?

4:30 P.M.
Waiting for Mum to come home so I can break the brilliant news.

5:00 P.M.
Phoned Jas. Her mum answered.

I said, "Hello, can I speak to Jas?"

I heard her shouting to Jas, "Jas, it's Georgia on the phone."

And I heard Jas shout back, "Can you tell her I'll talk to her later. Tom's showing me a new computer game."

A new computer game? Are they all mad?

If I had called down and said that a boy was showing me a computer game my bedroom would have been full of parents within seconds!!

Unless that boy was my cousin James, in which case I would have been left up there for years, because my family doesn't seem to mind incest.

6:30 p.m.
Mutti went ballisticisimus about the suspension. Even though I explained how it was not my fault and how provoked I was by Elvis.

When she calmed down she said, "Don't you think you might have a bit of a stomach bug?"

I said, "Here we go. Look, Mum, this is no time to be visiting Doctor Gorgeous. We should be thinking about Vati."

She said, "I AM thinking of Vati. And do you know what I'm thinking? I'm thinking that he'll go mad if he comes back and the first thing he hears is that his first born has been suspended. Now, are you feeling a bit poorly?"

My room
8:30 p.m.

Mum "suggested" I went to bed early and thought about the important things in life for once. She's right. I will think about the important things in life. Here goes:

My hair... quite nice in a mousey sort of way. I still think that a blonde streak is a good idea, even after the slight accident I had last time I tried it. The bit that snapped off has grown back now, but I notice Mum has hidden all the toilet cleaners and Grandad's stuff that he puts his false teeth in when he stays. She really is like a police dog.

Anyway, where was I? Oh yes, eyes... Nice, I think, sort of a yellow colour. Jas said I've got cats' eyes.

Nose... Yes well, it doesn't get any smaller. It's the squashiness I don't like. It doesn't seem to have any bone in it. I still can't forget what Grandad said about noses, that as you get older they get bigger and bigger as gravity pulls on them.

8:35 p.m.

You can make a sort of nose sling out of a pair of knickers! Like a sort of anti-gravity device. You put a leg hole over each ear and the middly bit supports your nose. It's quite comfy. I'm not saying that it looks very glamorous. I'm just saying it's comfy.

8:40 p.m.
It's not something I would wear outside of the privacy of my own bedroom.

8:45 p.m.
It's a good view from my windowsill. I can see Mr Next Door with his stupid poodles. He's all happy now that Angus has gone off poodle baiting in favour of the Burmese sex kitten.

8:46 p.m.
Oh hello, here comes BG, my ex, the breast fondler. At this rate he will be the one and only fondler. I will die unfondled. He must be coming home from football practice. I don't know how I could ever have thought about snogging him, he wears extremely tragic trousers. He is looking up at my window. He has seen me. He's stopped walking and is looking up at my window. Staring at me. Well, you know what they say – once a boy magnet always a boy magnet. I'm

just going to stare back in a really cool way. All right, Mr Big Gob, Mr Dumper. I might be the dumpee but you still can't take your eyes away from me though, can you??? I still fascinate him. He's just looking up at me. Just staring and staring.

Mesmerised by me.

8:50 p.m.
Oh my God! I am still wearing my nose hammock made out of knickers.

8:56 p.m.
Mark will tell all his mates.

8:57 p.m.
He will now call me a knicker-sniffer as well as a lesbian.

Midnight
Oh for heaven's sake! What now? Woken by loud shouting and swearing. Surely Dad is not home already? Looked through the window. It was Mr and Mrs Across the Road. They were hitting things in their garden, shouting and

shining torches. What on earth is the matter with them? This is no time for a disco inferno.

2:00 a.m.

Woke up fighting for breath from a dream about my nose getting bigger and bigger and my breasts getting bigger and bigger. And someone laughing and laughing at me. I couldn't seem to move anything except my head. Paralysis for being so horrid to Dave the Laugh. Libby was laughing like a loony. (Which of course she is.) She pulled my hair, "Look, bad boy!!! Aaahhh."

The weight was Angus curled up on my chest. Purring. I couldn't move, he weighs a ton. Big fat furry thing. I'm going to cut down on his rations. He's like a small horse.

Hang on a minute. He's not alone. He's got Naomi with him, curled up on top of him!!! Oh Blimey O'Reilley's trousers!

I managed to get them off me and they slunk off into the night – not before Angus had bitten my hand for my trouble. Naomi is a bit forward for a pedigree cat; she had her head practically up Angus's bottom as they went off.

I'll think about it in the morning. I mustn't do anything hasty. Like tell Mr and Mrs Across the Road.

Tuesday October 19th
8:45 a.m.

All hell broke loose. Mr and Mrs Across the Road came round "asking" about the Burmese sex kitten. Mr Across the Road had a spade and the words "Skinned and made into slippers" were mentioned. As she shut the door Mum said, "Honestly, Angus gets the blame for any bloody thing that goes on round here."

I said, "Yes... he's a scapewhatsit like me."

She said, "Shut up and get the balloons out."

Balloon city.
4:00 p.m.

The house is covered in balloons. I even made a banner for the gate, it says VELCOME HOME, VATI.

Libby has made something disgusting out of Playdough and bits of hair. She is wearing ALL of her dressing-up things: her Little Red Riding Hood outfit, fairy wings, deely boppers and, on top, her Pocahontas costume. She can hardly walk about.

No sign of Angus and Naomi. They will have made a love nest somewhere. Pray God my knickers are not involved in any way.

First of the loons arrive.
5:00 p.m.

Grandad almost broke my ribs; he's surprisingly strong for someone who is two hundred and eight. He gave me a sweet (!) and said, "Don't send your granny down the mines, there's enough slack in her knickers!!"

What is he talking about? Mum gave him a sherry. Oh good grief. That means he will take his false teeth out soon and make them do a "hilarious" dance.

6:00 p.m.
Excitement mounts (not). Uncle Eddie and Vati turned up on Uncle Eddie's pre-war motorbike. Vati leaped off the bike in a way that might have caused serious injury to a man of his years.

Mum and Dad practically ATE each other. Erlack!! How can they do that? In public.

I think Dad was crying. It's hard to tell when someone is as covered in facial hair as he is. He hugged me and went, "Oh, Gee... I... oh, I've missed you! Have you missed me?"

I went, "Nnnyeah."

Then Mum gave me a look and I pretended my stomach

bug was quite bad. We'd "agreed" that we would do the stomach bug scenario early on, so as not to arouse suspicion tomorrow morning. I was beginning to feel quite ill, actually. It's weird having him back. At least Mum more or less ignores me. Vati tends to take an interest in, well, exam results and so on.

7:00 p.m.

More and more people arrived. The drive was full of cars and old drunks. Mum and Dad were holding hands. It is so sad to see that sort of thing in people who should know better. I wondered if I should tell Vati he was in a love triangle with George Clooney. But then I thought no, can't be bothered.

12:30 a.m.

What a nightmare! All the so-called grown-ups got drunk and started "letting their hair down". Well, those of them that had any.

Uncle Eddie was spectacularly drunk. He put one of Libby's rattles with a sucker bottom on his head, to look like a dalek. Libby laughed a lot. Uncle Eddie was going,

"Exterminate, exterminate," for about a million years. But then Libby wanted it back and Uncle Eddie couldn't get the sucker off his head. All the drunkards had to pull on it together, and when it eventually came off Uncle Eddie had a round purple mark about a metre wide on his forehead. Which actually was quite funny.

1:00 a.m.

I went down to tell them that some of us were trying to sleep, so could they turn down Abba's Golden Hits, please. I saw them "dancing". God it was so sad. Dad was swivelling his hips around and clapping his hands together like a seal. Also he kept yelling, "Hey you! Get off of my cloud!!" like a geriatric Mick Jagger, and as Mick Jagger is about a million years old you can imagine how old and ludicrous Dad looked. Very old and ludicrous, that's how.

Mum was all red and flushed – she was TWISTING with Mr Next Door and they both fell over into a heap.

Wednesday October 20th

12:30 p.m.

Up at the crack of midday.

Mum in the kitchen in her apron making breakfast for us all. Oh no, sorry, I was just imagining being part of a proper family where that sort of thing happens. In Nicolson land the M and D are still in bed, even Libby was in there with them. I tried to get her to come into bed with me last night but she hit me and said, "No, bad boy, I go with Big Uggy!" (That's what she calls Dad – Big Uggy.) Angus was somewhere with the sex kitten and I was just... alone in my room. In my bed of pain. Because my ankle still hurt, not that anyone cared. Very, very alone as usual.

As alone as a... er... an elk.

You never see elks largeing it up with other elks, do you? They are always on their own, just on a mountain. Alone.

Ah well, I decided to take a Buddhist viewpoint and just be happy that everyone else is happy...

12:45 p.m.

Doorbell rang.

I called down, "The doorbell to your home is ringing."

♥ 225

No reply from the drunks.

The doorbell rang again. It would be Mr and Mrs Across the Road wanting to search the house for Angus and the Burmese sex kitten.

Ring ring.

I yelled as I hobbled down to answer it. "Don't worry about the fact that I have a limp and a very serious stomach complaint that makes me too sick to go to school... I will get up and answer the door. You recover your strength from lifting glasses up to your mouths!"

Silence. Well, just a bit of snoring from Libby.

I opened the door.

It was the Sex God.

At my door.

Looking like a Sex God.

At my door.

The Sex God had landed at my door.

I was wearing my Teletubbies pyjamas.

He said, "Hi."

I said, "Hhhnnnnngggghhh."

1:00 p.m.

I got dressed as quickly as I could. The Sex God said he would meet me by the telephone box so we could go for a walk round Stanmer Park. I dithered for about five minutes about lippy. I mean, if there is going to be snogging, is it worth putting it on? But then, if you don't put it on, does it look like you are expecting to snog, and is that too much pressure for boys who might go springing off in an elastic band way again?

Ooohhhh, I could feel my brain turning to soup. I knew I'd say something so stupid to the SG that even I would know it was stupid. That's how stupid it would be.

I didn't take any chances with the nipple department. I wore a bra and a vest. Let them get out of that if they could.

I must be calm. Om. Om. OhmyGodohmyGodohmyGod. My tongue seemed too big for my mouth. Do tongues grow? That would be the final straw if I had a tongue that just lolled out of my mouth. Shut up, brain!

1:25 p.m.

There he was, leaning against the wall! He was just so cool. His hair was flopping down over one eye.

♥ 227

When he looked up I went completely jelloid. He said, "Hi, Georgia. Come here."

And I said, "My dad has grown a little beard and I thought I was going to be lonely as an elk."

What in the name of pantyhose was I talking about? I'd be the last to know as usual.

The SG HELD OUT HIS HAND... to me!!!! Something I had dreamed of. Do you know what I did? I shook it!!!

He really laughed then, and grabbed hold of my hand. We walked to the park. Holding hands. In public. Me and a Sex God. I honestly couldn't think of anything to say. Well I could, but it would only have made sense to dogs. Or my grandad.

In the park we sat down on the grass, even though it was a bit on the nippy noodles side. Unfortunately I did feel like going to the piddly-diddly department, but I didn't say.

He looked at me for what seemed like ages and ages, and then he kissed me. It was all surf crashing and my insides felt like they were being sucked out. Which you wouldn't think was very pleasant. But it was. He put his hand on my face and kissed me quite hard. I felt all breathless and hot. It was brilliant. We whizzed through the scoring system for snogging in record time. We got to number four (kiss lasting over three minutes without a break), had a quick breather and then went into five (open mouth kissing) and a hint of six (tongues). Yesss!!!! I had got to number six with the Sex God!!! Again!!!

Eventually we had a bit of a chat. Well, he chatted. I just couldn't seem to say anything normal. Every time I thought of something to say, it was something like, "Do you want to see my impression of a lockjaw germ?" or "Can I eat your shirt?"

He had his arm round my shoulder, which was good because then he got profile rather than full-frontal nose. He said, "I haven't been able to forget you. I've tried. I tried to be glad when you started seeing Dave. But it didn't work. I even wrote a song for you. Do you want to hear it?"

I managed to say "Yes" without putting on a stupid French accent or something. Then he sort of pulled me backwards on to him so that my head was resting on his lap. It was quite nice, but I could see up his nose a bit. Which I didn't mind, because he is a Sex God and I love him. It's not like looking up Cousin James's nose, which would make anyone immediately sick. But then I thought, if he looked down and saw me looking up his nostrils, he might think it was a bit rude. So I settled on closing my eyes and letting a half-smile play around my lips.

Then he started singing me the song he had written for me. There weren't many words – it was mostly, "And I really had to see her again." And then melodic humming and yeahing. Unfortunately he was sort of jiggling his knees for the rhythm so my head was bobbling about. I don't know how attractive that looked.

4:00 p.m.

The Sex God has left the arena. He wants us to be, like, official snogging partners after my fifteenth next month. He's going to tell his parents.

I am irresistible.

I am truly a BABE magnet.

Even in my Teletubbies jimjams.

Even without mascara on.

Life is fabbity fab fab!!!!

Yessssss!!!!!! And triple hahahahahaha-di-haha!!!!

5:00 p.m.

M and D eventually got up. I didn't care because I am in the Land of the Very Fab, in fact beyond the Valley of the Fab and into the Universe of Marvy.

Vati is in a hideously good mood. He keeps looking at things and going, "Aahh-h" and hugging me. I wish he would get back to normal. I wonder how long it will be before he drops this "happy family" nonsense and gets all parenty.

6:00 p.m.
An hour, that's how long.

I was on the phone when it started. Telling Jas about SG. I said to her, "Yeah, come round and I'll tell you all about it. It is so FAB. How long will you be? OK. Good. Yeah anyway, he just turned up in his car. He looked BRILLIANT – you know those black jeans he has got, the really cool ones with the raised seam that..."

Vati had gone into the kitchen to get a cup of tea. He came out, stirring it. Jas had just asked me what sort of jacket SG was wearing and I was beginning to tell her when Dad interrupted and said, "Georgia, if Jas is coming round why are you talking to her on the phone? Phones cost money, you know."

Oh, I wondered how long it would be before the fascist landed. I said to Jas, "Have to go, Jas, I may already have wasted two pence. See you soon."

7:20 p.m.

In my room, daydreaming about my wedding. Can you wear black as a bride? Dad came up and suggested we have a family "chat". I know what that means, it means they tell me what they are going to do and expect me to go along with it, and if I don't they call me a spoiled teenager and send me to my room.

But I don't care any more. I said to Dad politely, "Look, why don't we just skip the boring middle bit where I have to come all the way downstairs and you tell me what to do and I say no I don't want to and then you send me straight to my room. Why don't I just stay in my room?"

He said, "I don't know what you are talking about. Come into the front room. And what's wrong with your eyes? They look all bunged up, have you got a cold?"

"It's Vaseline, it makes your eyelashes longer."

He said, "Can't you stop messing about with yourself?"

As I went downstairs I was thinking he should try messing about with himself a bit more. He never had what you might call good dress sense but it's so much worse since he's been in Kiwi-a-gogo land. Today he's wearing tartan slacks which is a crime against humanity in anyone's language. Also he has clipped his beard so that it is just on the end of his chin. No side bits and no moustache, just a beard thing... on the end of his chin. When we went in the room Mum kissed him on the cheek and stroked his beard... How disgusting.

Anyway, I don't care because I am going out with a Sex God and life is fab. I said, "OK, I am sitting comfortably. Rave on, El Beardo."

El Beardo said, "Great news!!! I've been offered a cottage in Scotland, I thought we would all go there for a week together as a family. Spend some quality time there together. Mum and Libbs, Grandad, Uncle Eddie, we could even ask Cousin James if you'd like a bit of company your own age. What do you think?"

Sacré bloody *bleu*. *Merde* and poo!!! Is what I think.

Fortunately the doorbell rang and Mrs Huge Knickers and me scampered up to my room. My room, which as usual, was full. Libby was in my bed with scuba-diving Barbie, Charlie Horse, Angus and Naomi.

I said, "Go play downstairs with Daddy, Libbs."

But she just stood up on my bed and started dancing, singing, "Winnie Bag Pool, Winnie Bag Pool." She got to the

♥ 233

bit where she takes off her panties, but I noticed they were suspiciously bulky, so I said, "Stop it, Libbs."

And she said, "Me let my legs grow."

"No, leave them on."

Too late. I thought Jas was going to faint. She doesn't have a clue what it's like to have a little sister. Me and Jas went off to the utility room for a bit of privacy. I was dying to tell her all about my snogging extravaganza, but she went raving on about Tom: "We went to the country."

Oh good Lord. Still I thought I'd better pretend to be interested otherwise I would never get to talk about myself. I said, "What for?"

"You know, to be on our own in nature."

"Why didn't you just go and sit in your room with some houseplants instead of tramping all the way to the country? You only snog there, anyway."

"No we don't."

"Oh yeah? What else do you do?"

"We looked at things."

"What things?"

"Flora and fauna and so on. Stuff we do in blodge. It was really interesting. Tom knows a lot of things. We found cuckoo spit and followed a badger trail."

I clapped my hands together and started skipping round the room. "Cuckoo spit!!! No!!! If only I could have come with you! Sadly there was a Sex God I had to snog."

Jas got all huffy and pink. It's hilarious when Jas gets miffed, and a reason in itself to make her irritated. She goes all red and pink apart from the tip of her nose which is white. Very funny, like a sort of pink panda in a short skirt and huge knickers.

She was all sulky, but then I put my arm round her. She said, "You can stop that."

I said, "I feel a bit sad though, because I'm so lucky and I can't help thinking about Dave the Laugh. He was a really nice bloke, and you know... er... a good laugh. It's sad that I have broken his heart."

Jas was poking around in Dad's fishing bag, which is not a good idea as he sometimes leaves maggots in there which turn into bluebottles. She said, "Oh, I meant to tell you. He's going out with Ellen. Tom and I are meeting them later at the pictures."

Midnight

Bloody *sacré bleu*. Dave the Laugh was supposed to really like me. How come he is going out with Ellen? How dare she go out with him? He is only just my ex.

1:00 a.m.

Still, I am going out with a Sex God. So I should be nice to everyone.

1:05 a.m.

Dave was a laugh, though. Even if he didn't make me go jelloid.

1:10 a.m.

I definitely go jelloid with the SG. Mmmmm, dreamy. But he doesn't make me laugh, he makes me stupid.

1:15 a.m.

I wonder if Dave the Laugh did that nibbling thing with Ellen?

1:20 a.m.

Looking through the window. Angus and Naomi are lurking

about on Mr and Mrs Next Door's garden wall. Angus is just dangling his paw down at the poodles. I hope there is not going to be group sex. (Whatever that is.)

1:25 a.m.
Perhaps I could have a jelloid boyfriend and an ordinary one for laughing with.

1:30 a.m.
Good grief! What in the name of pantyhose is going to happen next?!?

Georgia's Glossary

aggers · Agony. Like I said, no one has the time to say whole words, so aggers is short for agony. The unusually irritating among you might point out that aggers is actually longer than agony. My answer to that is – Haven't you got something else to do besides count letters?

billio · From the Australian outback. A billycan was something Aborigines boiled their goodies up in, or whatever it is they eat. Anyway, billio means boiling things up. Therefore, "my cheeks ached like billio" means... er... very achy. I don't know why we say it. It's a mystery, like many things. But that's the beauty of life.

Chrimbo hols · No one has the time to say long words, so Chrimbo is Christmas and hols is holidays. As in snog fest (snogging festival).

conk · Nose. This is very interesting historically. A very long time ago (1066) – even before my grandad was born – a bloke called William the Conqueror (French) came to England and shot our King Harold in the eye. Typical. And people wonder why we don't like the French much. Anyway, William had a big nose, and so to get our own back we called him William the Big Conk-erer. If you see what I mean. I hope you do because I am exhausting myself with my hilariosity and historiosity.

crèche · Kindergarten. Nursery. Playschool. Working muttis leave preschool children so they can "enjoy themselves" making things. A sort of day prison for toddlers.

dalek · In England we have this hilariously crap TV show called Dr Who where this bloke in a scarf goes time travelling. His archenemies are these senselessly violent creatures (no, not Angus surprisingly). They are called daleks. They're a form of robot. They have weird mechanical voices and a sort of gun sticking out of their head bits. They say, "Exterminate, exterminate!" Well, I told you it is crap.

DIY · Quite literally "Do It Yourself"! Rude when you think about it. Instead of getting someone competent to do things around the house (you know, like a trained electrician or a builder or a plumber), some vatis choose to do DIY. Always with disastrous results. For example, my bedroom ceiling has footprints in it because my vati decided he would go up on the roof and replace a few tiles. Hopeless.

duffing up · Duffing up is the female equivalent of beating up. It is not so violent and usually involves a lot of pushing with the occasional pinch.

geoggers · Geoggers is short for geography. Ditto blodge (biology) and lunck (lunch).

get off with · A romantic term. It means to use your womanly charms to entice a boy into a web of love. Oh, OK then – snogging.

gob · Gob is an attractive term for someone's mouth. For example, if you saw Mark (from up the road who has the biggest mouth known to womankind) you could yell politely, "Good Lord, Mark, don't open your gob, otherwise people may think you are a basking whale in trousers and throw a mackerel at you!" Or something else full of hilariosity.

goosegog · Gooseberry. I know you are looking all quizzical now. OK. If there are two people and they want to snog and you keep hanging about saying, "Do you fancy some chewing gum?" or "Have you seen my interesting new socks?" you are a gooseberry. Or for short a goosegog, i.e., someone who nobody wants around.

gorgey · Gorgeous. Like fabby (fabulous) and marvy (marvellous).

Jammy Dodger · Biscuit with jam in it. Very nutritious (ish).

jelly rabbit · Jelly made into a rabbit shape. Children like this sort of thing. You make some jelly and pour it into a rabbit-shaped mould. When it is set the child amuses itself by eating its bottom with a spoon. Or scooping out its eyes. Or, in Libby's case, by placing it in my bed.

Knickers · Amercians (wrongly) call them panties. Knickers are a particular type of "panty" – huge and all encompassing. In the olden days (i.e., when Dad was born) all the ladies wore massive knickers that came to their knees. Many, many amusing songs were made up about knicker elastic breaking. This is because, as Slim, our headmistress, points out to anybody interested (i.e., no one), "In the old days people knew how to enjoy themselves with simple pleasures." Well, I have news for her. We modern people enjoy ourselves with knicker stories, too. We often laugh as we imagine how many homeless people she could house in hers.

jimjams · Pyjamas. Also pygmies or jammies.

lippy · Oh come on, you know what it is! Lipstick!! Honestly, what are you like?!

loo · Lavatory. In America they say "rest room", which is funny, as I never feel like having a rest when I go to the lavatory.

mincers · Cockney-type people in London use rhyming slang so that other (normal) people will not know what they are talking about. I don't know why – that is the beauty of the Cockneys. Mincers is short for mince pies, which rhymes with eyes. Get it?

Neighbours · A really crap daytime soap opera set in a suburb in Australia. Kylie Minogue was in it.

nub · The heart of the matter. You can also say gist and thrust. This is from the name for the centre of a wheel where the spokes come out. Or do I mean hub? Who cares. I feel a dance coming on.

nuddy-pants · Quite literally nude-coloured pants, and you know what nude-coloured pants are? They are no pants. So if you are in your nuddy-pants you are in your no pants, i.e., you are naked.

panstick · Stick of makeup that you use to cover up spots with. Or in my mutti's case to cover up the ravages of time and a careless attitude to skin care.

physio · A sort of massage. Short for physiotherapy. For instance, if you had a muscle that really, really hurt and that you wanted left alone, a cruel person (Miss Stamp) would insist on giving you a violent pummelling to make it better. Ha.

rate · To fancy someone. Like I fancy (or rate) the Sex God. And I certainly do fancy the SG, as anyone with the brains of an earwig (i.e., not Jas) would know by now. Phew – even writing about him in the glossary has made me go all jelloid. And stupidoid.

Reeves and Mortimer · Are a comedy double act. They are very mad indeed. But I like them.

rucky · A rucksack. Like a little kangaroo pouch you wear on your back to put things in. Backpack.

shirty · Flustered and twitchy and coming on all pompous.

Slack Alice · A Slack Alice is someone who is all stupid and nerdy. The sort of person who is always pulling their knickers up because they are too big (i.e., Jas).

umby · Umbrella. Also "brolly". Mary Poppins used to say "gamp" for umbrella. But what I say to that is – who cares?

wet · A drippy, useless, nerdy idiot. Lindsay.

whelks · A horrible shellfish thing that only the truly mad (like my grandad, for instance) eat. They are unbelievably slimy and mucuslike.

P.S.

Turn the page for a peek at my next book...

FABULOUSLY FUNNY BESTSELLER

'Knocked out by my nunga-nungas.'

You'll laugh your knickers off!

Louise Rennison

www.georgianicolson.com

Return of the loonleader

Thursday October 21st
1:00 p.m.
Looking out of my bedroom window, counting my unblessings. Raining. A lot. It's like living fully dressed in a pond.

And I am the prisoner of whatsit.

I have to stay in my room, pretending to have tummy lurgy, so that Dad will not know I am an ostracised leper banned from Stalag 14 (i.e. suspended from school). I'm not alone in my room, though, because my cat Angus is also under house arrest for his love romps with Naomi the Burmese sex kitten.

2:00 p.m.
They'll be doing PE now.

I never thought the day would come when I would long to hear Miss Stamp (Sports *Oberführer* and part-time lesbian) say, "Right, girls, into your PE knickers!"

But it has.

3:30 p.m.
All the Ace Gang will be thinking about the walk home from school.

Applying a touch of lippy. A hint of nail polish. Maybe even mascara because it is RE and Miss Wilson can't even control her tragic 70s hairdo let alone a class. Rosie said she was going to test Miss Wilson's sanity by giving herself a face mask in class and see if Miss Wilson has a nervy spaz.

Jas will be practising her pouting in case she bumps into Tom.

3:50 p.m.
How come Jas got off with cloakroom duty and I got banned? I am a whatsit... a scapething y.

4:10 p.m.
Robbie the Sex God (MY NEW BOYFRIEND!!! Yesss and three times yesss!!!!!) will be going home from college now. Walking along in a Sex Goddy sort of way. A walking snogging machine.

4:30 p.m.
Mutti came in.

"Right, you can start making your startling recovery now, Georgia."

Oh cheers. Thanks a lot. Goodnight.

Just because Elvis Attwood, school caretaker from Planet of the Loons, tripped over his own wheelbarrow (when I told him Jas was on fire) I am banned from school.

Mutti rambled on, although she makes very little sense since Vati got home.

"It's your own fault, you antagonise him and now you are paying the price."

Yeah yeah, rave on.

4:45 p.m.
Phoned Jas.

"Jas."

"Oh, hi Gee."

"Why didn't you phone me?"

"You're phoning me. I would have got the engaged tone."

"Jas, please don't annoy me, I've only been speaking to you for two seconds."

"I'm not annoying you."

"Wrong."

"Well, I've only said about two words to you."

"That's enough."

Silence.

"Jas?"

Silence.

"Jas... what are you doing?"

"I'm not annoying you."

She drives me to the brink of madnosity. Still, I really needed to speak to her, so I went on. "It's really crap at home. I almost wish I hadn't been banned from school. How was Stalag 14? Any goss?"

"No, just the usual. Nauseating P. Green smashed a chair to smithereens and back."

"Really?! Was she fighting with it?"

"No, she was sitting on it having her lunch. It was the jumbo-sized Mars bar that did it. The Bummer Twins started singing "Who ate all the pies?" to her but Slim, our beloved headmistress, heard them and gave us a lecture about mocking the unfortunate."

"Were her chins going all jelloid?"

"Yeah. In fact it was Chin City."

"Fantastic. Are you all missing me? Did anyone talk about me or anything?"

"No, not really."

Charming. Jas has a lot of good qualities though, qualities you need in a bestest pal. Qualities like, for instance, going out with the brother of a Sex God. I said, "Has Hunky – I mean, Tom – mentioned anything that Robbie has said about me?"

"Erm... let me think."

Then there was this slurp slurp noise.

She was making slurping noises.

"Jas, what are you eating?"

"I'm sucking my pen top so I can think better."

Bloody *sacré bleu*, I have got *le idiot* for a pal. Forty-nine centuries of pen-sucking later she said, "No, he hasn't said anything."

7:00 p.m.
Why hasn't Robbie mentioned me? Hasn't he got snogging withdrawal?

8:00 p.m.
I can hear Vati singing "If I Ruled the World". Good Lord. I have only just recovered from a very bad bout of pretend lurgy. He has no consideration for others.

8:05 p.m.
The worsterosity of it is that the Loonleader (my vati) has returned from Kiwi-a-gogo land and I thought he would be there for ages. But sadly life was against me and he has returned. Not content with that he has insisted we all go to Och-aye land to "bond" on a family holiday.

But... na-na-na-na-na and who-gives-two-short-flying-pigs'-botties? because I live in Love Heaven.

Lalalalalalala.

I am the girlfriend of a Sex God!!!

Yesss!!! Result!!!!